VERTICAL WORLD ∀

THE VEILS OF CTHONIA

BY BRIAN CRAWFORD

EPIC Escape

An Imprint of EPIC Press
abdopublishing.com

The Veils of Cthonia
Vertical World: Book #2

abdopublishing.com

Published by EPIC Press, a division of ABDO, PO Box 398166, Minneapolis, Minnesota 55439. Copyright © 2019 by Abdo Consulting Group, Inc. International copyrights reserved in all countries. No part of this book may be reproduced in any form without written permission from the publisher. Escape™ is a trademark and logo of EPIC Press.

Printed in the United States of America, North Mankato, Minnesota.
052018
092018

♻

Cover design by Christina Doffing
Images for cover art obtained from iStockphoto.com
Edited by Gil Conrad

Library of Congress Cataloging-in-Publication Data

Library of Congress Control Number: 2018932902

Publisher's Cataloging in Publication Data

Names: Crawford, Brian, author.
Title: The veils of Cthonia/ by Brian Crawford
Description: Minneapolis, MN : EPIC Press, 2019 | Series: Vertical world; #2
Summary: Sent by their command to the Ætherians' water-extraction site, a group of ten Cthonian scouts travels for days across the desert. Their mission: to find water for their drought-afflicted civilization. But when two of the scouts' bodies plunge to the ground from above, the plan changes—and one enraged Cthonian commander strikes back.
Identifiers: ISBN 9781680769128 (lib. bdg.) | ISBN 9781680769401 (ebook)
Subjects: LCSH: Drought relief--Fiction. | Survival--Fiction--Fiction. | Revolutions--Fiction--Fiction. | Science fiction--Societies, etc--Fiction | Young adult fiction.
Classification: DDC [FIC]--dc23

This series is dedicated to Debbie Pearson.
Thank you for everything.

ONE

ELEVEN DAYS BEFORE TÁTEA'S POWER WORKS erupted in a ball of flame and smoke, a group of ten Cthonian spotters plodded east across the scorching desert far below. Their goal: to reach the struts supporting the stratospheric colony of Ætheria. Their mission: to find water.

Moving her body in time with her sauntering eqūs—a large, horse-like animal—Aral kept her eyes fixed on the horizon. The darkening yellow clouds told her evening was approaching. Maybe in another hour it would be dark. Even though neither she nor anyone else in Cthonia had ever seen the sun, the permanent cloud cover reassured her in its regularity and predictability. Dark was night; soft glow, morning; dim glow, noon; steady glow, early afternoon; softening glow, late afternoon; dimming, evening. The pattern never changed. Even in Cthonia's frequent acid storms, the level of diffused light remained constant.

No one in the ten-person group talked, and they had silenced their radios. Any extraneous sounds would get in the way of their eyes and ears, which were probing every square mile of the landscape, looking and listening.

"We know they're out there," Cthonia's command had said before their assignment. "We knew even before we had our Ætherian informant to give us specifics when she fled from *up there* sixteen years ago. According to her, they have a constant source of water; and right now, ours has dried up. That's all that matters. They are drawing water up from the ground through some massive tube. There must be water underground. Right below their colony. How else could they be surviving? You need to find it and drill. They may just be a tribe of cloud-dwellers keeping to themselves, but maybe they can help, too. Maybe they can share some water in the meantime, just long enough to give us time to find some of our own. You need to find out."

Aral worked her swollen, dry tongue around her mouth, trying to generate some spit. She wanted to make her small supply of concentrated water blisters last. The size of golf balls, these small, transparent pouches provided the same hydration as four gallons of water; one could hydrate a person for two days. She winced. Moving her jaw caused her cracked lips to sting and bleed. She knew she shouldn't lick them, but she couldn't help it.

She tried to distract herself by lifting her binoculars and scanning the wasteland around her. Her eyes darted left and right across the magnified image. The drab, depressing forms of rocks, acid-resistant cacti, plateaus, buttes, and outcroppings danced in reddish tones, filtered through thermal infrared. Nothing.

Again. Aral emitted a sardonic titter under her breath, thinking of the meaning of the word "desert." Empty. Deserted. That's what she was looking at. That was her world—everything beyond her isolated settlement of the Cthonian Cave Complex, the CCC. A desert.

She lowered the binoculars and took a deep breath. She fought off the nagging worry that grew with each step. Back in the CCC, her people were depending on her and her team to find water. Her parents were depending on her. Her friends. With the CCC's underground aquifer suddenly dry after eight hundred years of supply, everyone knew it was just a matter of weeks before people in their self-sufficient enclave would die. They couldn't count on rain; it was too acidic. And in two weeks, their tanks would be empty, and thousands of people would perish. Dead in the middle of the parched desert of Cthonia.

"Patrol, stop." Tell, the leader of her team, called back to the others. "We'll set up camp here."

Three eqūs ahead, Tell pulled his mount's reins and turned his steed around to face his team. Aral pulled her reins as well. Ferda, her eqūs, spat and snorted. The sweating animal turned her head and glared at her with a bulging, questioning eye. *Will there be water here?* she seemed to ask. Aral looked down and patted the base of her neck.

"Not here, girl, not here. But maybe we're close . . ." she whispered. She and her nine-person team had brought enough water blisters to sustain the eqūs and themselves, but not enough to let any of them thrive.

She looked up at the mountain range, which loomed closer but was still several miles away. From where she stood, she could make out the entrances to hundreds of little caves—four- to eight-foot-wide pockmarks eroded into the ground by centuries of acidic rain.

As she dismounted, Aral concentrated on hiding her worry from her eqūs, who always picked up on her emotions. She knew that if they didn't find water soon, the animals would suffer and die before they could make it back to the CCC. What news would they bring to those who expected so much of them?

Aral sat up straight and peered at the churning yellowish cloud that hung low over the wall of mountains facing them—the same unending cloud she'd seen every day of her sixteen years on Cthonia. One that had blocked out the sun and strangled most of Cthonia's plant life, turning the planet into a barren wasteland.

"I wonder . . . " she said and patted her eqūs on the rump. Her eyes fell on the six-inch-wide branding that marked Ferda's bulging muscle. It was the same as the tattoo on every over-sixteen's upper arm in Cthonia:

$$\underline{\nabla}$$

—

"Alright, team, let's go over this again," Tell said, wedging a foot-long rock under his bottom as a seat.

He crossed his legs and pulled out a small metallic clipboard. The other nine patrol members sat in a circle around him. Although there were ten in their group, they had twelve eqūs in their cortege. The two extra ones carried mining and water-finding supplies: hydrosensors, drills, humidity sensors, echolocation transmitters, pipes . . . Hopefully, with this equipment, the team would be able to scout around the base of the Ætherians' water tube to locate another source. Hopefully, a sustainable one . . . one that could provide for the entire colony. And if so, they would radio back for reinforcements to come mine it out and begin construction of a hydropipeline all the way back to their cave settlement.

In the middle of the group, a two-thousand-lumen lantern threw stringent, bluish-white light on the others' faces, making them even paler than they already were. Behind Tell, the patrol's large, pop-up tent flapped in the late evening breeze. Off to the left, the twelve eqūs lingered at their tethers, attached to five metal spikes driven into the ground.

"We've covered a hundred miles in three days," he said, his eyes dancing over his notes. "I just radioed back to CCC. No news."

"Still no water?" Aral asked.

Tell shook his head.

"No—drought's still on. Food supply back in the Cave Complex seems to be okay for now, but soon people are gonna run out."

"Even the fungus?" Aral asked, referring to the underground, edible fungus the Cthonians cultivated deep in the caves. Thanks to the greenish, bitter but calorie-packed mold, the Cthonians had been able to survive as long as they had. It was the only food anyone could grow, and it fed both people and eqūs.

He paused, glancing over his notes.

"The misters have dried out," he answered Aral's naïve question. "No humidity, no fungus. No fungus, no food. Besides, there's still no clue as to why the aquifer dried out."

"How much longer?" Estrella asked. Aral looked at her friend. Of the other members of the team,

Estrella, at seventeen, was closest in age to Aral, being one year older. The others were all in their late teens or early twenties, the age deemed most agile and resilient for active spotting, according to command—especially in Cthonia's hostile environment. Before joining the contact party, Estrella and Aral had spent years together back at the CCC learning, practicing, and mastering dressage, riding, and eqūs jumping. Aral had even become the pride of her parents with these skills, all of which had grown important to the Cthonians' survival over the years, as sources of cthoneum gas had evaporated over the past hundred years, making gas-powered transportation useless.

"We should have enough water and food for another day," Tell answered, looking up. He glanced back toward the eqūs, whose eyelids drooped. "Enough for us and the animals and to get us back, in case," he said. "But assuming we *do* find it, the CCC will send motorized backup for digging."

"How will we know when we get there?" Aral asked.

Tell straightened his back and looked up. "We've seen it before. Well, not me, but others. We'll know we're there when we come across a bunch of wires and poles that, according to the informant, we'll find if we follow the coordinates she gave us."

Everyone in Cthonia either knew the informant or heard of her: Máire Himmel—the only Ætherian in living history to ever make contact with the Cthonians. Sixteen years ago, she'd appeared to a team of Cthonian spotters checking for signs of water sources other than their aquifer. When they'd found her wandering in the desert, they didn't know who she was, but they knew that she was different: she was about a foot shorter than any Cthonian; her thorax was much broader; and her skin was much darker than any Cthonian's, whose skin appeared pale in comparison . . . sickly, even.

At the time, she'd said she was escaping *up top*. There, someone called a Head Ductor was keeping oxygen from the people, who had to survive in a hypoxic environment. Shortly after she had a baby son, she'd been forced to flee, leaving the boy behind. Her life was in danger. Ever since, she'd lived with the Cthonians and helped monitor water extraction and distribution. Because she'd been so skilled at rationing oxygen up above, she held the skills to watch over Cthonia's limited water supply. A few years after she arrived, Cthonia's command also had her teach classes on Ætheria so that, according to the command, "young Cthonians can have an appreciation of the last barbaric tribe of Cthonia." From her lessons, young Cthonians learned, above all, that Ætheria was filled with sluggish pale-skins who kept to themselves and bickered over oxygen, and that she had a son named Rex whose face was partly paralyzed from birth. If the Cthonians remembered any name from her disheartened ramblings, it was Rex. To the Cthonians, Máire had become one of them.

And now that their water had dried up, Máire was able to direct them to Ætheria's base, where the cloud-dwellers had been siphoning up groundwater for centuries.

TWO

THE FOLLOWING DAY WAS HOT—MUCH HOTTER than the days before. As the procession worked its way to, then into, then up the mountains, the heat tore at Aral's eyes, face, and lips, baking her alive. Though all she had to do was hold on and keep her eyes forward, her body throbbed from thirst, fatigue, and the endless up-and-down, up-and-down, up-and-down of Ferda's muscular back.

Ka-clump, ka-clump, ka-clump . . . The eqūs wheezed as they pushed their way up the mountain pass, their shod hooves slipping and scraping over brittle rock. The incline wasn't too steep, but Aral found herself worrying more and more about her animal. Tell had said they'd had enough water blisters to make it out and back, but how much more of this desiccated journey could Ferda take? And Aral?

She was ready to go home. She was ready to get back to her friends and back to training. But she was also ready to stop having to worry about water.

The eqūs pushed higher and higher. Aral soon became aware of another painful sensation—her back. All of the team members wore message pods—foot-long, oblong-shaped backpacks that contained data recorders monitoring the wearer's heart rate, blood pressure, oxygen saturation, and fluctuations in VO2 uptake—all through a series of sticky sensors placed over their backs and chests. In addition to measuring bodily functions, the sensors were attached to the wearer's headset and chest microphone, recording anything the wearer said. On Aral's right forearm, a red button slumbered just below the elbow. In case of emergency or accident, all Aral had to do was press the button and the pod would launch from her backpack and land a half mile away—away from danger. Because it was fitted with a homing device, others from the CCC would could find it and analyze the circumstances surrounding her "accident," should she have one. But now, sweltering in the heat and leaning forward to avoid falling, Aral's monitor pads were rubbing her skin raw. With each lurch of her eqūs, she grimaced. No matter how much pain she was in at the moment, patrol rules prevented her from pulling off the sensors.

"How much farther?" Aral asked through her headset, her eyes fixed on Tell's undulating back ahead. He rotated his head over his right shoulder and shot her a look. He didn't answer right away. He turned forward and Aral could see him lift his binoculars to his face and gaze up the slope of the mountain.

"Another mile?" he said as a question. "Hard to see from here."

"Okay."

After another two hours, the jagged, rocky path they were following angled up to the left and fell in line parallel to the mountain ridge. For another half mile, the team trundled northward, the trail keeping them twenty yards or so under the summit. They could have stopped, dismounted, and walked up, but Tell never gave the order. As they gained in altitude, the midday heat was tempered by an increasing wind as the air on the mountain's westward side slammed into the rocky slopes and rushed upward, cresting at the summit and launching high into the atmosphere.

Aral looked up. The boiling yellow cloud hung closer than she'd ever seen it—maybe two miles. Its bulges created upside-down rifts and valleys that shifted like waves. When she'd been much younger, she used to lie outside with Estrella and cloud-gaze, each of the girls trying to catch a glimpse of something—anything—that might hover high above the clouds. They were looking for a gap in the billowing formations that might let some sun through and allow them to glimpse for once—just once—what they'd read and heard about in so many bedtime stories of what Ætheria was like long, long ago. But by the time the girls had turned ten, they'd begun to accept the reality: Cthonia was covered by this thick cloud, and it would always be covered. Why dream of what was impossible?

The trail straightened out, cresting on the mountain ridge and stretching northward. The twelve eqūs fell into line on the summit. The Cthonian landscape opened up on both sides of the mountain. Aral prodded her mare to go faster and worked her up to the front of the line—next to Tell. A soft breeze blew against the team from the west, providing some respite from the searing heat.

Aral leaned to the left to peer ahead. In front of Tell, the path continued down the length of the ridge. If she looked left, she could see the mountain's entire westward-facing slope easing down into the twenty-mile-long plain they'd just crossed the day before. If she looked to the right, she saw the eastern face of the mountain crumbling down in giant, jagged outcroppings like enormous, decaying teeth.

She pulled out her binoculars and, still riding,

scanned the landscape to her right. It was much harder to keep focused amid the rocking and shaking from Ferda's shoulders. Through her eyepiece, the grayish rock and dirt swooped and swished across her field of vision at dizzying speeds, forming a whirlwind of undefined lines and swirls.

She saw something.

"Stop!" she snapped—not so much a shout but a firm command. She pulled Ferda's reins and the animal stopped and snorted.

"What is it?" Tell's voice trickled back.

"There's something out there."

"What?"

"There," she said. "Look through your binoculars. That way."

Keeping her eyes locked onto her binoculars, Aral heard the eqūs behind her shuffle to a stop.

With Ferda standing in place, Aral stood in the stirrups and twisted her body to the right. She turned the focus knob with her right middle finger. The horizon's contours sharpened, and she was able to get a clear view of the thing that had caught her attention. According to the binoculars' internal distance gauge, the horizon sat ten miles away. The air was breathable, and the ambient temperature hovered at ninety-four degrees.

But there, at that ten-mile point, the horizon's monotony was broken by something stretching up from the ground. From this distance, it looked to be a gigantic pylon or tube that the binoculars rated at twenty yards wide. Its exterior was reddish and uniform, and its lowermost extremity was anchored into the ground. The other end disappeared into the clouds, which hovered miles above Cthonia's surface.

Aral lowered her binoculars and squinted, jittery excitement filling her body. Without the powerful lenses, she now saw that with the naked eye and from this distance, the thing looked like some sort of string hanging from the cloud. Unless you were staring straight at it, it would've been easy to miss. Which was no doubt why Tell and the others hadn't seen

it at first. Aral shuddered. She knew she was looking at Ætheria's support structure and its water pipe.
She'd heard about it many times in Máire's class, but
now that she saw the outpost, she felt almost elated
at seeing something so unusual for the first time and
elated that the Ætherians—if there were still any up
there—might be able to help them solve their water
problem.

Her breath came in short bursts. Her heart
pounded. She felt she was observing something big.
Something life-changing.

Aral looked left and right at the other nine in the
patrol. They were all staring slack-jawed through their
binoculars. They had seen it, too. Aral wondered
if the same nervous emotions were swarming her
teammates.

"Look at that!" Estrella said. "Look on either side
of the pipe-thing. There's something else. Something
more. I wonder if that's the supports Máire told us
about."

Aral pulled her binoculars back to her eyes and

located the pipe. It stood impassably, indifferent to the world around it, like some kind of massive monument or statue. She squinted and teased the focus knob.

On either side of the pipe, stretching out for several miles in either direction, a network of dozens of smaller poles spanned the distance between Cthonia and the cloud, disappearing into the billows above. It was like a surreal, metallic forest of infinitely high trees that had neither branches nor leaves. Unlike the pipe, which was about twenty yards across, these were smaller than a foot wide. From this distance, she couldn't tell their exact size. But as she examined the network of pipes, she soon realized that there were many more than she'd thought. There must've been hundreds.

Aral lowered her binoculars and glanced at her teammates. Half of them still gazed at the pipes, half looked toward Tell. She too looked to Tell. His face had gone paler than usual. He lowered his binoculars and looked back in Aral's direction.

"There they are. We've found them."

"Do you think anyone still lives up there?" Aral asked.

"Hmm," Tell said. "Chances are good. According to Máire, there were one or two thousand still up there. But that *was* sixteen years ago. Anything could've happened. We'll just have to see."

"Have any other Cthonians ever come here?" Aral asked.

Tell shrugged.

"A few times, yes. At least that's what I've been told, but that was before my time. It's so far away and not worth it. There's just nothing here. And I think when they came it was before Máire even came down. So at least with her, we have better directions. But as far as I know, no Cthonians has come this far into the wilderness in years."

"Isn't it dangerous up there?" Aral asked, her curiosity getting the best of her.

"I imagine," Tell said. "Máire had always said people had less energy because they couldn't breathe,

or something like that. And that it's freezing cold."
He looked up at the impenetrable cloud cover. "She
also mentioned that oxygen had been a problem, and
that's why she came down but . . . " He trailed off.

As Aral gazed at the pipes, her initial exhilaration
turned into a strong desire to see the pipes up close.
She wondered what the Ætherians were like, if they
were still alive. Would their homes be at the top of
those stilts? Where did those stilts end? Surely not
in the cloud . . . But over it? Did they have a view of
the sun?

She looked over at Tell.

"What do we do?" she asked. "Apart from those
poles, I haven't seen any signs of water anywhere."
She stared at her leader, who sat focused on analyzing
the pipes.

"Well, their water's going to be in that pipe, if
they're still pumping it up," he said. "Our job is to
scan the area all around for signs of any more underground." Tell then lowered his binoculars and slid
them into their case on his belt. He reached for his

radio transmitter, which was clipped to the left side of his binoculars case. He held up his finger to Aral as if to tell her to wait. He lifted the transmitter to his mouth and pressed the transmit button.

"Triple C One, this is Tell in Patrol One, just beyond the Eastern Quadrant."

"Yes, we hear you, Tell. Triple C One here. Your report?"

Tell looked at the others, his lips closed tight.

"Triple C One, we've arrived at the bottom structure of the Ætherian complex. We have found it."

"We didn't catch that, Tell. What do you see?"

"Triple C One, I repeat: we have found the Ætherian structure."

"Good news, Tell! Is it the water pipe?"

"It looks like it, yes. From here, all we can see is metallic stilts leading from the ground up into the clouds. Just like the Ætherian said. There's also one that's much bigger. That must be the water pipe."

There was a silence. What was the radio controller doing on the other end? Reporting to the command?

Waiting for instructions? Checking intelligence reports?

While the team waited for base to answer, the ten spotters shifted from staring at the pipes, to looking at Tell for some clues as to what he was thinking, to stroking their eqūs. Aral trembled in anticipation. The mounting easterly wind whipped around them, creating an otherworldly howl.

"Tell, are you there? This is Triple C One."

Tell raised the transmitter to his mouth. "Tell here. Go ahead."

"We have clearance for you to proceed. Get down to the pipe and determine if there is water present in the pipe, which will mean there are still surviving Ætherians. If so, radio in for further instructions. You will also need to begin your scouting for water in the area of the pipe. But we don't want to disturb their water source. If the Ætherians are up there and are extracting water, we don't want conflict, just water. This is a peaceful mission. Do you understand?"

"Got it. Standby for contact when we reach the pipe."

THREE

BEFORE THE TEAM HAD LEFT THE CCC, mechanics in the complex had begun servicing the Cthonians' few remaining combustion vehicles to bring mining and digging equipment, assuming they would find signs of water. This was the first time Aral could remember anyone even mentioning the machines, much less preparing them for use.

In all, the Cthonians stocked ten overland rovers; two low-altitude, swivel-reactor aircrafts; and one heavy-duty, all-terrain cargo transporter. Aral had once heard of the Cthonians trying to fly years before, but the pilots and mechanics were too nervous to use the centuries-old relics. Before the Cthonians' reserves of cthoneum gas began to dry up, the planes and automobiles had been grounded, while eqūs had been brought back into use—there had been no other choice. The settlement still maintained reserves for emergencies, however.

And apparently this was considered an emergency. The airships were the only viable means for transporting the Cthonians' mining and water-drilling equipment—the same equipment that allowed them to dig and develop their cave network eight centuries before.

The team worked their way down the jagged, rocky eastern side of the mountain range. Because the terrain was so much wilder than the western side, it was nearly dark when they reached the gentler foothills. After hours of negotiating the perilous footholds, Tell led the group to a secluded alcove, where they would be protected from the wind.

The team set up camp and watered their eqūs. Night fell, and the ten members were exhausted and jittery. *What was going to happen? Were the Ætherians still alive? Máire had said they were all in need of oxygen; maybe they were all dead? But if they were alive, would they know the Cthonians were looking for water right below them?* Too many unanswered questions hung in the air, but everyone was jumpy with the excitement of being so near a new world.

As she ate in the white light of the group's lantern, Aral found herself glancing westward, squinting up the side of the black mountain range. This was the farthest she'd ever been from the Cthonian Cave Complex. Even when riding around back home with Estrella, they'd never wandered farther than a mile or two away. CCC rules forbade anyone from venturing out into the desert. "There's no water, no food, and if it rains, you'll be stuck in a bath that will be pretty uncomfortable," she'd been told in some form by every adult in the complex—especially her teachers, including the Ætherian Máire. "When I first came down," she'd told her students in their Ætherian History class, "I got caught in the rain. I've never felt my skin itch so much. I was lucky to run into a Cthonian patrol who brought me back."

When she'd finished eating, Aral stood and walked to Ferda, who was tethered with the others. As she approached, she noticed that her eqūs was holding her back left foot slightly off the ground, avoiding putting any weight on it.

"What's wrong, girl?" Aral said. The eqūs turned her head and eyed Aral imploringly.

Aral leaned over and lifted Ferda's hoof. Even in the dim light of the lantern, she could see the oblong shape of a marble-sized rock that had become wedged between the animal's hoof and shoe.

"Oh, why didn't you tell me earlier?" Aral said, pulling out a small knife from her utility belt. She rotated her back towards Ferda's head and pulled the eqūs's hoof up between her legs. Working with firm but gentle movements, she wedged her blade between the rock and the shoe and twisted, working the rock loose.

"You know your eqūs." Tell's voice surprised Aral. Without looking up, she continued her work.

"Yeah. I guess."

"Tired yet?" Tell asked.

With a grunt, Aral popped the rock from Ferda's hoof. It landed on the sand with a *plop*.

"It is what it is," she said, standing. "It's good being on an eqūs, I guess."

"Hmm. Well, try to get some rest. We've got a lot more work tomorrow." He paused, as if deciding whether he should continue. "And don't wander off."

Aral felt a pang of anger. "That was only *once*," she said. "And I wasn't trying to run away or anything. I wasn't even a spotter, then." Her thoughts drifted back to when she had been fourteen and just learning to ride. Despite the rules, she had wandered miles out into the desert, lost in the fantasies of what lay beyond. By the time she'd come back, a team had already been sent out to look for her. She'd almost lost all riding privileges, and the stunt had gained her the reputation of being stubborn and, when she'd argued with the irate commander of the search party, quarrelsome. Still, she'd only been fourteen then, and the command didn't hold it against her when she joined the spotters with the other sixteen-year-olds. But the reputation stuck.

"No need to get snappy," Tell said. "I know you were younger and I get it: you like to explore. Just stay with us and stay safe. We're a team."

"Got it."

As Tell turned and walked back to the group, Aral squinted towards the pipes. Her imagination once again began to flare.

—

The following morning, the sun woke the team with a searing heat and air that felt drier than usual. The patrol members stirred, ate in silence, and prepared their packs.

Jittery with what lay ahead, no one spoke during the ride across the plain. No one spoke—but everyone seemed to read each other's thoughts. Tell kept his eyes forward, but the others—Aral, Estrella, and the rest—fidgeted in their saddles between eyes front, taking our their binoculars and trying to get a closer glimpse of their goal, shooting meaningful glances at each other, and adjusting their positions atop their equs.

Like massive but faraway prison bars, the network of pipes inched toward them at a snail's pace. One moment Aral would find the parallel vertical lines to be dancing in the heat of the growing morning like a desert mirage. Laughing, unchanging, the pipes leered at her, always seeming to stay the same distance away, no matter how far they rode. She might look back at Estrella, who rode just behind her, and when she turned forward again, the pipes had jumped up in space, looming larger than before. There was no continuity in their movement, only jerky, spastic jumps.

Aral took a water blister. She bit through the edible skin, felt the water swish around her dry mouth, and swallowed. *That should hold for a day in this heat*, she thought. She looked at her watch. Just after nine in the morning. They'd already been riding for an hour.

Up ahead, Tell looked forward with his binoculars, lifting himself off of his saddle as he did so to steady himself. He sat back down and put the instrument away. He turned his head over his right shoulder and cupped his left hand around his mouth to shout.

"Just a mile left! Let's make it a gallop!"

Midway through his last sentence, he tapped his eqūs's sides with his feet. The animal responded, swelling her pace to a gallop. Aral admired the eqūs's strength and stamina. You wouldn't have known just from looking at her that Tell's mare had spent the last few days walking almost nonstop.

Following Tell's lead, the others spurred their eqūs on. As Ferda sped up, Aral breathed in, allowing the rush of oncoming air to cool her sweat-covered face and neck. She felt her bun unraveling at the eqūs's jostling, and soon her hair—which, unbound, hung to the middle of her back—was whipping behind her like a kite's streamers. She lifted her rear from the saddle and absorbed the gallop with her legs, *ka-clump, ka-clump, ka-clump, ka-clump.* The more the animal trotted forward, the more her thighs burned from effort. But Aral smiled as much as her chapped lips allowed; she enjoyed these workouts, and she often took secret pride in running her hands over her legs, which after years of eqūs riding and jumping had become rock-hard.

Her heart beat faster. Up ahead, the pipes loomed larger—so much so that she could discern more details than she had seen before.

All around the thick main pipe, a forest of smaller ones—which now looked more like poles than pipes—glistened in the yellowish light cast down through the never-ending cloud above. They were clearly made of some sort of metal, though what Aral couldn't say. *Titanium? Aluminum?* Whatever it was, it had to be extremely light. For the sheer mass of the poles—however thin—was enough to weigh several tons each. At soil level, they were planted in what appeared to be concrete anchors fitted with

T-receptacles. The poles, each about the diameter of Aral's wrist, were lodged and bolted in place. From there, they stretched, unending, straight up, where they disappeared into the perpetually churning cloud several miles up. Aral followed the poles up with squinting eyes, but she could see no joints. The pipes were perfectly smooth, as if they had been produced by some massive machine that squeezed the pipe out like giant strands of pasta. *But how would they hoist it up?* she thought. *The only way would be with some kind of high atmosphere airship or something that could hover above the clouds.* She couldn't imagine how these gigantic pipes could be made, let alone anchored in place.

"Watch out! Cables all around!" Tell shouted back. His voice stirred Aral from admiring the metallic forest. She looked down, ahead, and all around. When she saw what was rushing at the team, a twinge of fear gripped her, but she realized that Ferda was doing a better job than she at navigating what had become a type of minefield.

Now within five hundred yards of the poles, Aral ducked her head and clenched the eqūs between her thighs. The team had entered a dense network of inch-thick guy wires, each bolted to iron anchors in the ground and each stretching upward at an angle toward the cloud. The wires were everywhere; as Ferda galloped around and through them, they whipped and swooshed and snapped all around, threatening to clothesline Aral and throw her to the ground. As she pulled herself closer to her mount, she glimpsed the others in front of and behind her. They were all doing the same, trying not to be yanked from their animals.

Aral pulled Ferda's reins to slow her. The animal heeded. Now moving at a safer pace, Aral looked around and realized that the wires pointed up and toward what she assumed to be the tops of the poles, hidden beyond the clouds. The poles still stood about three hundred yards away. *Those must be supporting whatever's up top,* she thought, at the same time trying to imagine what Ætheria could look like and remembering her Ætherian history lessons from Máire back in school. How big was it? How high? Were there actual buildings up top, as Máire had taught them, or something else? She tried to look more closely at each wire as her eqūs moseyed by. Each one seemed still, stable. *Whatever is at the end of those pipes must be pretty solid.*

When the team had cleared the wires, Tell spurred his eqūs to a gallop. The others followed. Within two minutes, they had reached the main tube.

Tell reined his eqūs to a stop and dismounted. The others fell in line with him and hopped to the ground.

"Careful everyone," Tell said. He stepped up to one of the support poles and placed his hand on it. He leaned forward and examined the structure.

Turning away from him, Aral also stepped up to a pole, slowing her pace as she neared it, awestruck. This was no ordinary pole. Not only were there no joints visible in its entire length, but its surface was reflective—more so, even, than a mirror. In the pole, Aral saw a lengthened, distorted image of herself

41

approaching cautiously, reaching out her hand to make contact.

She laid her hand on the metal. She gasped. Unlike every metal she'd ever encountered, this one did not absorb her body heat, giving the impression that it was cold. It seemed to adopt the exact temperature of her hand, and this made it feel almost as if the strut were not even there—as if it were visible but not tangible. Its warmth gave it a softness, a familiarity and strength that made her feel as though she could trust it with her life . . . even several miles above Cthonia's surface.

"You should take a look at this." Tell's voice caused Aral to jump. She turned to her left, where he had left his pole and moved over to the larger tube—but not before tying his eqūs to one of the poles. Aral looked back at Ferda, patted her neck, and wrapped the eqūs's lead around the mysterious pole. Ferda's eye bulged at her, confused.

"Don't worry, girl, I'm just over there." She smiled and walked to where Tell stood.

Aral stepped up to the gargantuan tube and admired the construction. *This must be the water tube Máire had told us about*, she thought.

The tube was twenty yards in diameter. Unlike the poles, it was dark red. It was peppered with rivets winding up its entire expanse, which plunged into the boiling yellowish cloud high above. Unlike the poles, its base was not anchored in cement foundations. Rather, it disappeared directly into Cthonia's surface. On one side, what appeared to be an access door rose from about two inches above the ground to a height of six feet—short enough that any Cthonian entering would have to duck. The door contained no handle, latch, or visible hinges. It appeared to open from the inside, and it did not budge when Aral pushed against it.

Aral squatted and ran her fingers around the base, where metal met soil. She pushed some of the dirt out of the way and dug a few inches. The pipe continued down, uninterrupted. *How deep did it go? And to where?*

Aral stood and placed both hands on the tube. Like the poles, its temperature was the same as her hands. With her hands still on the tube, she leaned forward and looked up. Like a colossal highway, the pipe stretched upward in two parallel lines descending on a common point—a point hidden somewhere beyond the cloud. As she gazed upward, she realized her body felt almost numb. She'd never seen anything this unearthly—this mammoth—in her life.

And then she froze. Something was happening. Or rather, she felt something—something in her hands. Something strange.

She held her breath and listened, concentrating on the feel of the metal under her palms. In her ears, only the sounds of the desert wind, her teammates' footsteps, and the eqūs' snorts and nickers danced about. She heard nothing out of the ordinary. But when she didn't move, when she held her breath, she could feel it. Straight through her palms, up the length of her arms, and into her shoulders.

The tube was vibrating.

At first she doubted what she felt. She focused again. This time, there was no doubt. Like some giant monster emitting a low snarl from the depths of its gullet, the tube seemed to be growling, gurgling, churning.

She glanced at her teammates, some of whom were also looking at the tube, but all on the same side. None of them seemed to have noticed the rumble. Her heart pounding, she leaned her head in and placed her right ear on the metal. Slowly, carefully, she eased it flat, almost to the point of forming suction between the metal and the helix of her ear.

GRRRRRRRBRBRBRBBBBRB.

With her ear pressed against the tube, the sound was unmistakable—deafening, even.

Something was happening. It was as if the tube were alive. Which meant . . .

"Tell! You guys! There's something inside!" Aral shouted. "Listen!"

No sooner had she finished speaking than the others became animated with nervous energy. Their movements were jerky and erratic. On either side of her, the nine others drew closer to the tube, placing their hands and ears on it just as she had done.

"Oh, my God," Tell said, jumping back from the tube as if he'd been bitten. "It sounds like . . . "

"It's clearly operational," Aral interrupted, finishing Tell's thought. As if to suggest through mime what she was thinking, she raised her head skyward.

"There must still be people up there," Tell said. Aral looked at her leader. All color had faded from her face. The others let out gasps as wonder set in—wonder and relief that they might be close to finding water for their civilization. "Máire wasn't sure if this was still working," Tell continued. "No one was. But if that sound is water, then they must be up there. Let's check. Jackson!" Tell called out to one of the spotters who'd been at the rear of the train.

"Yes?"

"Bring me a hydrosensor. I need to see what's in here."

"Got it!" Jackson trotted to one of the

46

supplies-carrying eqūs and rummaged through a compartment on its pack. He withdrew a small black protective case, which he unzipped. He pulled out a device that looked like a small metal detector attached to a handheld monitor and brought it over to Tell. The group's leader took the hydrosensor and pressed a button on its side. The monitor blinked to life, as did a small blue light on the side of the device. Tell stared at the glowing monitor, which cycled through several screens. The blue light switched to green.

"Let's see, now," Tell said, stepping up to the pipe. Holding the monitor in his left hand, he raised the device's sensor and placed against the dark red metal. Almost instantly the monitor flashed a barrage of numbers. Tell's face brightened.

"That's it," he said, excitement in his voice. "There is moving water in there. About a thousand gallons a minute. That's a lot. And it's mineral content is high. No pollutants. To be pulling up that much water, the Ætherans must've tapped into a huge source." He lowered the sensor and stepped back, raising his head as he eyed the length of the pipe. Almost instantly, the team began to talk amongst themselves, their elation palpable. Not only were they right underneath a colony of people no Cthonian had seen in nearly a thousand years, but they were just within reach of water . . . which meant salvation.

"Water's being pulled up, all right. Which means they're still up there . . . and, most likely, alive." He shifted his eyes from the pipe to the sand all around. He seemed to be scanning for surface irregularities or breaks in the sand—anything that might indicate the nature of whatever might lie hidden underground.

"Okay, team," he said, his voice trembling at the thrill of discovery. "We're not done yet. Each of you grab a hydrosensor, and let's spread out. We'll work in concentric circles, starting twenty yards out from the pipe. Work your way around, and let's see what we can see. Take measurements every five yards. C'mon, let's go."

One by one, the team shuffled up to the supply eqūs, pulled out hydrosensors, and began to spread out. Their movements were energetic, shaky even, which marked a dramatic change from the monotonous torpor of the past two days.

"Good luck," Aral said to Estrella as her friend headed off toward the tube, hydrosensor in hand. Estrella winked and smiled, turning on the device as she walked.

When her turn came, Aral reached in to the second supply eqūs's pack, where the electronics were kept, and pulled out one of the remaining cases. She walked over to a spot about fifty yards from the water tube, unzipped the pack, and pulled out her hydrosensor. Before turning on the device, she glanced around. Five of the other spotters had already begun scanning the ground like treasure hunters searching for clues. Each person held their eyes transfixed on their monitor screens.

Aral turned on her hydrosensor and glanced at the screen as the device awoke. This would be her first time using one of the delicate instruments on an actual assignment. Back during their mission briefing at the CCC, she'd practiced, but only to locate bottles of water that Tell had hidden just under the sand. Now, her work was real.

Aral lowered the sensor to just inches over the ground and paused, allowing the hydrosensor to take a reading. Because the ambient light in Cthonia was always diffuse and yellowish, it was easy to make out the figures on the screen. While the device scanned, a series of three dots flashed in sequence, indicating to the operator to wait. Then, a disheartening message appeared:

H2O confirmed: **NO**

Aral lifted the sensor and walked forward five yards. She repeated the process, only to receive the same message. Again and again she worked her way forward, her heart lurching with each flashing dot and each negative message. *How could there be no water?* she wondered, casting a sideward glance at the massive pipe, which was sucking up enough water surely to sustain Ætheria and Cthonia. *How deep was their source? How far underground did that pipe actually go?* She tried to fight off the unease that grew with each step and each scan. Unease began to morph into fear: What if they had come this far only to have the water stay just out of reach? Then what? Would they ask the Ætherians to share? Would the Ætherians even be friendly to them? What if Máire's fleeing sixteen years before had created some kind of hostility towards the Cthonians? She had always said that she'd been persecuted and forced to flee. What if the Ætherians would use water as a means to get revenge?

Aral shook off her fears as she caught her imagination spinning out of control. None of her fears were based on fact, she realized, just dreams and nightmares . . . ones that had become even more intense since the disappearance of Cthonia's water a week before.

Around her, the other spotters continued their search without talking. By now, Aral had worked her way halfway around the pipe, creating a semicircle of footsteps a hundred yards in diameter. She was about thirty yards ahead of the others, who waited longer than she did at each scanning point. Maybe it was her natural impatience that drove her ahead so fast, or maybe it was her growing worry they'd find nothing. But in either case, she didn't see the point in staring at the hydrosensor's monitor every few feet, as if it would suddenly change its mind and deliver a different reading other than "H2O confirmed: NO." With each step, Aral grew more frustrated.

At the next five-yard mark, she let the sensor drop onto the ground and swore under her breath. Rather than watch the monitor for the reading, she looked up and at the eqūs, which were now almost a hundred yards away. They were either sniffing the ground for something to eat or looking around with what she imagined to be bored expressions. Aral was pleased to see that, even from this distance, Ferda was looking in her direction. She'd ridden that eqūs for the past two years, and she'd grown attached to the animal. She wondered if Ferda could see her from that distance. She liked to think the two had a bond they could feel even when they were separated and couldn't see each other. She tried to make out Ferda's eyes, but at that distance, the eqūs's brown hair blended in to form a featureless expression. Only when her eqūs looked away did Aral look back at the hydrosensor's monitor. She froze at what she saw.

H2O confirmed: **YES**	Forecasted indefinite
Depth of source:	Mineral content:
819 feet	Ca2+ 38%
Temp: 5° C	Mg2+ 7%
Stagnant/Eddies/	Na+ 12%
Flowing	Cl .002%
Current @ 321 gal/min	Sulfates 30 mg/gal
Sustainability:	Other/unidentified 1%

"Tell!" Aral shouted, her heart pounding in her ears. "Here! I've found it! There's water underground!"

FOUR

"**T**RIPLE C ONE, TRIPLE C ONE, THIS IS TELL. DO you hear me?" Tell pulled the receiver away and glanced to the others, who were chattering excitedly as they circled the spot of Aral's discovery. Every few feet, they placed their hydrosensors on the ground in an attempt to delineate the edges of the water source.

"Tell, this is Triple C One, what's going on?"

Tell sprang to life. He pulled the receiver back to his mouth. In clipped and rapid-fire words, he spat into the radio everything the team had discovered: the poles, the guy wires, the pipe, the rumble, and most importantly, the water . . .

"It's the Ætherians," he finished. "There's water being drawn up through their pipe. They must still be there. *And* we've found more water underground! It's about sixty yards from the tube. The only guess I can make is that the tube goes very deep, and we've found an upward bulge in the aquifer or whatever's down there. Sensors show that there's a lot. The sustainability forecast is even at 'indefinite.' This could be it."

A silence. It felt as if the responders at the CCC were calling a meeting right then to discuss the meaning of the team's confirmation that the Ætherians were still there and that there was more water.

"Tell," the voice crackled through the radio.

"Yes?"

"Orders from direction are to remove yourselves a half mile from the pipe and set up camp. The mining and reconnaissance team will arrive within ten hours. We have to establish an extraction operation. But to do that, we need to reach out to the Ætherians to negotiate. We're going to make contact."

———

Aral didn't sleep that night.

After Tell's communication with the CCC, the team pulled back and set up camp. The tents were much slower to rise than usual, because the team's attention was split between their work and looking back at the humming tube that disappeared into the cloud. As for Aral, her body buzzed with anticipation and fear. She had heard so many stories—legends—about the Ætherians while growing up, but she'd never dreamed she would come this close to their civilization. She felt like an explorer who'd spent her entire life wandering the endless, impenetrable jungle in search of a lost tribe and had finally found it. She was giddy, speechless, and nervous all at once—not a good combination for getting sleep in the middle of an arid, hostile environment in the shadow of a hidden society. Added to this was the giddiness that Cthonia's water problems might be nearing a solution.

Since she'd joined the Cthonian Spotter Force, Aral had never had problems adapting to the tough environments her explorations took her and her fellow spotters to. In the year since she'd joined, she'd slept in tents, in the open, and in caves. But now, now that so much was happening, the sandy ground felt rock-hard, and her sweat clung to her body, sleeping bag, and tent side, causing her clammy flesh to peel away from the cloth every time she turned over or shifted position. Her thoughts swam, and images of what the Ætherians might be like danced through her mind. Some of the Ætherians were friendly. Some were suspicious. Some were hostile. But all were new—new and unique, different from the Cthonians in their language, their dress, their behavior, and their . . .

A penetrating rumble snapped Aral from her sleep. She sat up and wiped her eyes, realizing she must've drifted off. She looked around. Darkness. A light nighttime wind caused the sides of the tent to flutter. Somewhere in her tent, a lone mosquito buzzed with a high-pitched squeal.

That wasn't what had woken her. She froze, listening. *There*. She jerked her head to the side. There was no doubt. As the wind shifted, it brought with it the far-off growl of motors. Machines. An airship. They were coming: CCC's mining and reconnaissance team.

With jerky movements, Aral yanked on her utility top and wedged her feet into her tight-fitting boots. She pulled her headlamp over her head and pressed the on button, filling the tent with searing light. Hands trembling, she snapped the hooked velvet flaps over her shoes and scrambled to free herself from her tent. She jerked open the door zipper with a *zzzzz-ziiiiippppp!* and flung herself into the chilly night. She stood up straight and breathed in a lungful of cool air. She glanced at her watch: 4:22 a.m. Dawn would come soon.

Outside, Tell was already up and jumping from tent to tent, waking the others with repeated, "Up! Come on! They're here." No sooner would his voice pierce through the slumbering silence of each tent than Aral would hear rustling, clipping, snapping, and zipping from the insides. The spotters were springing up at Tell's calls.

"I'm up!" Aral shouted. In between tents, Tell stood, nodded at her, and continued to wake the others. Aral turned to her right and saw Estrella's familiar form walking over in the dark, her silhouette obscured by the glare of her headlamp.

"Did you hear it?" Aral asked as her friend stepped up.

"Yeah," Estrella nodded toward the west. "That way. Look."

Aral turned toward the direction they'd come from and peered into the night. She reached her hand up and turned off her headlight to let her see better in the dark. With her light off, she scanned the horizon in an attempt to regain her night vision. She soon saw that night vision wasn't necessary.

About two miles away, a pair of white aerial lights hovered over the landscape as a massive air-ship approached, one light on each wing. The lights floated a few hundred feet up and were rapidly approaching. What had started as a distant rumble grew into a combination of high-pitched whine, low growl, and explosive internal combustion. The lights grew closer, and soon Aral noticed something else underneath the flying machine: flame. Constant spurts of bluish-orange flame shot out toward the ground in lengthy isosceles triangles.

"What is that?" Aral asked Estrella. "Do you see the fire?"

Estrella shifted in place and emitted a *hmpf.*

"Those are the jet engines," she said.

The machine approached. Aral and Estrella took several steps back. It roared closer, its shiny, silvery fuselage glittering with the white, orange, and blue reflections of the light coming from the blaring engines. The light bounced off of the brownish sand, causing the behemoth to emerge from the darkness like a giant, screaming creature flying through the night.

Aral's heart bounded. Until now she'd only seen

Cthonia's two remaining airships in storage at the CCC, but she'd never seen one in operation. Rumor had it they hadn't been used in decades, if not centuries. It was amazing to behold and like nothing she'd ever seen.

The airship's fuselage was about forty yards long by ten yards wide, making it seem fat and ungainly in the sky. Its wings were disproportionately wide and stumpy, each about twenty yards long from the airship's body. The tip of each wing clutched a massive, circular jet engine that roared louder than anything Aral had ever heard. As the airship approached its landing site, the two engines rotated so that their wash went from pointing backwards to pointing down. This allowed the airship to take off and land in a relatively small space. Aral assumed it needed no lengthy runway to gain speed before taking off. The engines were powerful enough to lift the monster straight up; and once at a satisfactory height, the engines would rotate slowly, pushing the airship forward.

Now about a hundred yards away, the airship

lowered into position for landing . . . closer, closer, closer . . . *Lucky*, Aral thought, *they're just outside of the guy wires. Can they even see the wires and the struts?* As the two engines rotated, both Aral and Estrella covered their ears and squinted their eyes. This let them protect their eyes from the storm of biting sand particles that the wash threw up all around them like a miniature sandstorm. Aral turned her face away from the stinging sand that spat and slashed at her exposed skin. Behind them, the twelve eqūs whinnied and neighed, yanking against their tethers to break free. But the poles and their reins held fast.

"Clear! Let's go!" Tell's voice shouted above the din. Hearing her leader speak through her plugged ears, Aral removed her hands and looked back toward the planes, which had now settled their rubber talons onto the ground.

The howl of the two motors decreased in pitch and slowed in intensity. The pilots had killed the engines. As they wound down, the sandstorm abated and

Aral could open her eyes and look westward without having her eyes scarred by hurtling sand particles.

Tell had broken into a run. It was as if he were trying to reach the airship before its motors had fallen silent.

Aral, Estrella, and the others followed.

Pumping her arms as she ran, Aral kept her eyes on the airship. Within a minute of landing, the engines had become silent. Now the only sound emerging from the machine was a low hum, as if it were idling, trying to save energy. In the cockpit, Aral could see the shapes of two pilots leaning forward in their seats and moving their hands across a hidden control panel. A soft glow from the invisible dashboard lit their angular faces. She could not make out their eyes, which were covered by darkened goggles, but she could tell that they were scanning their controls and powering down the giant craft.

When they had reached within twenty yards of the airship's front, the team paused. Aral's chest heaved from running. In front of her, Tell stood statue-still.

His shoulders and arms were motionless. He didn't seem out of breath. Aral glanced to her right. Estrella had kept up with her, and the two exchanged meaningful looks before turning back to the airship. *Can you believe this?* they seemed to say to each other through their intense gazes.

Crack! Hisssssss! Underneath the fuselage, a downward-facing hatch popped and slid open. One end remained affixed to the airship's belly, while the other pivoted downward, its descent controlled by a hydraulic cylinder on either side that emitted a high-pitched squeal as it moved. Before the door's edge had touched the ground, Aral saw several pairs of booted feet working their way from inside the airship and down the ramp. It was as if whoever was inside couldn't even wait for the airship to be fully stopped before getting out. The ramp planted its end into the sand and the clumping boots revealed legs, then torsos, then bodies. Three men and three women, all wearing the uniform of the Cthonian Spotter Force, marched down and out of the airship.

Without stopping, they headed straight for Tell. Still blinded by the piercing glow of the aerial lights, Aral couldn't make out the people's faces, only that they were uniformed.

Tell stepped forward and extended his hand. The tallest man in front of the six-person group reached out and shook it. Aral stepped forward to within earshot. Tell glanced around, his headlamp casting white light on the man's face. Aral recognized him as Brondl, the commander back at the CCC who'd originally given the spotters their orders to head to Ætheria's water pipe.

"Nice job," Brondl said, shaking Tell's hand. Brondl looked up at Aral and the others. From Tell's original group, Jackson stepped up to Brondl and the two hugged.

"That's his son," Estrella whispered to Aral.

"Really?"

"Uh-huh. Like father, like son, I guess."

"Good work to all of you!" Brondl shouted over the airplanes' purr. "You are all part of history. You should know that." He stepped to Tell's side and brought his hand to his eyes to squint into the dark. Aral followed his stare. She noticed the first light of dawn was glowing dark yellow in the east—it was still dark out, but the dawn was just light enough to make out the thick, black shadow of the tube about a mile away stretching from the ground to the cloud.

"Now," Brondl continued. Aral turned back to the commander. "We just need to figure out what course history will take next."

FIVE

THE NEXT DAY BUZZED WITH FRENZIED activity.

In addition to mining supplies, the airship brought a team of thirty members of the Cthonian Spotter Force, as well as the materials to construct a mobile operational base inside the network of guy wires and within yards of the massive tube. Before nightfall, the Cthonians—including Tell's team of ten—had erected a field tent large enough to plan and coordinate an investigative expedition to make contact with the Ætherians. They also erected several annex, dormitory tents to shelter all forty of the spotters from the elements. The tents' footprints were about the size of circus tents', but the ceiling of the command tent—at five yards' height—was much lower.

At the center of the bivouac, Brondl and his five-person entourage set up a control hub. They installed nine folding tables in a large rectangle, which they covered with unrolled maps, charts, and graphs, as well as stacks of books that contained reams of pages documenting the history of Cthonia since the Separation—when different groups of people had fled Cthonia's deteriorating atmosphere centuries before by either settling in massive caves (which was what the Cthonians had done) or constructing sky-high colonies above the clouds (the Ætherians). Around the tables, they strung a garland of constantly glowing lights that made the center meeting point of the tent burn with a pale bluish white.

Along the right side of the tent, the spotters neatly arranged piles and piles of sturdy, black metallic gear boxes that contained all manner of mining materials, surveillance equipment, power tools, such as saws and micro-sanders, respirators, oxygen containers and auditory detection devices, plus food and water blisters. In the smaller tents, the spotters installed rows of folding cots and personal footlockers. The pit latrines were to be outside the tent, on the opposite side of the main door, which faced the guy wires and the tube.

In just nine hours, the spotters had set up a small, self-contained village of forty inhabitants.

Throughout the tent's assembly, Brondl remained in radio contact with the CCC. Though Tell remained responsible for coordinating his ten spotters, he was no longer the voice of authority. All spotters now deferred to Brondl, who made his presence felt through his imposing physique, piercing eyes, and booming voice. As the troops worked to get their settlement ready for action, he seemed to be everywhere—overseeing, commanding, supporting, encouraging, laughing, scrutinizing, inspecting, planning, and pacing. He was up in the morning before anyone, and he lay down for sleep only after everyone else had relaxed into slack-jawed slumber . . . everyone but two guards who remained on patrol outside all night.

With the command post in place, Brondl called the first assembly. The forty spotters crowded around the tables, each person working their way around everyone else so that all could have a clear view of Brondl, who stood at the end of the table. Aral was able to work her way up to one of the tables and secure a seat for herself. Estrella had not been so lucky. She stood three rows behind her friend. Aral folded her arms on the table in front of her and listened as Brondl spoke.

"Thank you again for your hard work." Brondl paused, looking around the crowd. Aral had the feeling he was trying to make eye contact with every person. His eyes lingered on Jackson's before he continued. "When we sent you out, we honestly didn't know what you'd find. After all, all of our intelligence about this area has come from one person, the Ætherian refugee. It would've been best to bring her here as well, so she could share her knowledge in a more direct manner as we negotiate next steps. But command felt it would be too dangerous for her, given her status as a refugee and asylum seeker. Still, she supplied us with ample intelligence to proceed."

Brondl took a deep breath and continued.

"And so here we are. This is a momentous day. Thanks to the hard work of Tell and his spotters," he gestured to Tell, who stood several yards to Brondl's left, "we have a chance to get our water back *and* reach out to the Ætherians. From what you have found already, it looks like we've found enough water for both of us. We now have two main goals. First, command has decided it would first be best to reach out to the Ætherians, for two reasons. On the one hand, we need to see if we might share some of their water from the tube while we dig our own well, which should take some time. Second, we have to begin our own extraction here, where the water source seems strongest. Basically two straws drawing from the same cup. Now we need to see if they can help. Maybe share? We also need to communicate to them that our work here is peaceful, and that we don't mean to encroach on anything they feel belongs to them." Brondl pointed straight ahead and up, indicating the tube and the poles, which stood more than a half mile away outside of the tent.

Aral raised her hand.

"Yes?" Brondl asked.

"Why would they share with us? And what about what Máire the Ætherian said? That they're hostile."

Brondl nodded. A murmur went through the crowd.

"Yes, we've thought of that. According to Máire, there's very little oxygen up there. Our hope is to use that to negotiate. They let us have water, we let them have oxygen. If they agree, we can bottle it and send it up." He paused, looking at the massive pipe. "That is, assuming we succeed at getting up. But one thing at a time."

"How's that going to work?" Tell asked.

"According to the Ætherian, the inside of that tube

is not just water. There are several pipes inside. One draws up water, another the explosive cthoneum gas, and a third, carbon dioxide. The rest of the tube is open, and contains a series of maintenance ladders that go all the way up. Every fifty yards or so, there's a platform. This should allow us to climb up and rest as needed along the way. Because that climb's at least several miles up. All we need to do first is get inside the tube.

"So, while you've been getting the command post up," he continued. "I have been in constant contact with the CCC about the next steps. We're going up." He pointed upward.

"But there are problems," he continued. "We don't have anything that will let us see or hear up through those clouds. As far as using the airship is concerned, there are just too many unknowns: how thick those clouds are, how stormy things are in there, whether we'd even be able to get the airship up and through . . . " He trailed off. "As it is, this is the first time in sixty years we've even moved her," he gestured in the direction of where the airship was parked, "and the flight over was bumpy enough. We also never got higher than several hundred feet. No, there are just too many risks. If we lose her, then we lose everyone inside, as well as one of our only two airships—this one, and the one still parked at the Cave Complex. No . . . " He paused, lost in thought.

"So the only way is to send people up. It's the safest way."

There was a murmur around the table. Some of the spotters exchanged worried glances.

"Tomorrow morning, we are going to try and cut open that tube to access the ladder. While you were setting up, I also inspected the tube and conducted a thorough auscultation of its perimeter. I found the side where the water and gas pipes are. We'll cut into the hollow side and climb up. Each spotter will of course have their ComPod on their back." Aral nodded, thinking of her own ComPod, whose sensor pads had rubbed her skin raw on the journey over. In addition to recording the wearer's speech and vital statistics, the ComPod also contained a homing device in its support frame, which hugged the wearer's back. This meant that the location of the wearer could be tracked even in case of a ComPod ejection.

"And so our plan," Brondl continued, "is for our spotters not only to go up, but while up there, to try to carry a message from us so that we can make contact with whoever's up there and negotiate for some water while we dig." Brondl paused and looked at Jackson, who seemed about twenty years younger. "And I'm particularly proud of the team who will be going up, because my own blood will join them!" He pointed at his son, who smiled and nodded. "So we are all invested fully in this mission's success."

SIX

THE TEAM BEGAN DUAL PREPARATIONS AT once.

On the one hand, the majority of the spotters would install the mining equipment above the shallowest detected water source and begin drilling. But with the water at eight hundred feet down, reaching it could take weeks, especially if bedrock was in the way. The team had brought explosives for this, but their first line of attack was to use their diamond-tipped drill to work down as far as they could. Using the explosives would be tricky and dangerous—tricky, because they would have to get the charges all the way down a small tube and detonate them from a distance and dangerous because no one on the team had experience actually using the explosives, which were leftovers from the creation of the CCC used hundreds of years before.

As for the ascent group, this would consist of six spotters, all of whom had much more experience than Aral. Their plan was to enter the tube at ground level and attempt an ascent. Based on Máire's calculations, the Ætherian complex sat between five and six miles up. "One hell of a climb," Brondl had said as he'd designated the six to go up. "But I can't think of any spotters stronger or more capable, that's for sure." He'd smiled as he'd patted his son on the shoulder. "They're going to make us all proud. All of Cthonia, even!"

As the ascent team assembled its gear, Aral's job was to double-check and inventory each item they'd be taking up. Her list was in turn triple- and quadruple-checked by two other spotters falling in behind her. There could be no mistakes . . . especially when six spotters' lives could be at stake. Who knew how harsh the conditions were above the clouds? They had to have functional gear to protect them, and the gear could not malfunction.

Darkness fell. It stretched through midnight and into the early hours of morning. The tent buzzed with activity. Just to the left of the command post table, an array of gear had been laid out in order. Aral stepped up with a metallic clipboard and checked each item. Her instructions were to first read the name of the piece of gear from her checklist, look at the gear, touch it, check it off, and then repeat the name of the gear before moving on. It all seemed a little obsessive to Aral, but orders were orders, and Brondl's mantra was "no mistakes, no matter what."

Eyes stinging from fatigue, Aral worked through the list for each of the six spotters, item by item: head-lamp with extra bulbs and batteries; radio transmitter; recording pod; connecting wires; carabiners; utility belt; utility gloves; utility knife; particulate mask that covered the mouth and nose ("We don't know what's in that cloud," Brondl had said); three water blisters—good enough for three days' hydration; energy gel; helmet; and personal first aid kit. Everything was there. Everything was in good order. Everything was ready.

When she'd finished the inventory, she delivered her form to Tell, who'd been watching from near the tables.

"All set?" he asked.

"Yes." She turned and looked back at the gear. The other two spotters had just finished their inventory and brought their forms to Tell. He nodded for the two to be dismissed and compared the three forms. Sensing that Aral was still standing there, he held up his hand for her to wait. He looked up and scanned the tent, looking for someone among the bobbing heads of the other spotters and technicians.

"Brondl!" Tell shouted, having found who he was looking for. Aral turned in the direction Tell was looking. The general was talking with six spotters, all of whom seemed in their late teens. Three were girls;

three were boys. Aral recognized Jackson among the group. These were the six who'd be going up. Brondl must've been briefing them, but he looked up at Tell's shout and nodded, his eyes saying, "What is it?"

"The gear's ready, sir."

"Checked four times?" Brondl asked, projecting his voice over the noise.

"Yes, sir."

Brondl nodded and turned back to the spotters. Aral saw him say something else to them, but she couldn't hear his voice. He nodded to each and then pointed behind him to where the gear lay. The spotters nodded back and trotted over to the organized piles. One by one, they lifted each piece of gear and strapped it to themselves—either around their waist, on their back, or on their head. Aral watched them get ready, part of her burning with envy to see what they were about to see. What would it be like up there? Even though she couldn't go up, she'd at least had a hand in getting their gear ready. For now, that would be as close as she would come to going above the clouds.

"Now what?" she asked, turning back to Tell. She was surprised to see his eyes were already on her.

"Tomorrow we'll help out with the digging. But for now, you can go to bed if you want. It's past midnight. Right now they're opening up the tube."

"Wait—right now?" Aral felt a surge of excitement. "Can we go see?"

"You mean the tube? Now? Outside?"

"Yes." She looked imploringly at her group leader.

Tell looked around. The six spotters were now fully suited up and walking toward the tent door. Some of the other spotters lingered or trickled out with them.

"Don't you want to sleep? Who knows what they'll find or what tomorrow—I mean, today—will bring. You look like you need the rest."

"Thanks," she said sarcastically. "With everything going on, I just wanna see, actually. I'll go to bed after they cut it open. Okay?" She opened her eyes wide in an attempt to look more awake and alert than she felt.

Tell raised his eyebrows. "Well, I don't think there'll be much to see, but sure. Let's go."

The two followed the six spotters outside. Up ahead, Aral could see Brondl's red hair bobbing in front of the others. The group walked slowly, calmly, as if in no hurry. As she left the tent and entered the transit tube leading out from the command center, she noticed that others were tagging along as well. The only people to remain behind were a few who stumbled off to bed and seven technicians who huddled over blinking computer screens at the tables. *They must be monitoring the ascent spotters' ComPods,* Aral thought, peering at the shiny, black packs attached to each of the six spotters' backs.

As the group approached the water tube, Aral heard an increase in the sound of activity. As the six spotters had been preparing back in the tent, another team had taken up position around the base of the tube. When they reached the end of the transit tube,

Brondl, the spotters, and the onlookers spread out over the sand, giving plenty of space to the six spotters huddled around the base. Aral stepped aside and watched them as they worked.

The six seemed oblivious to their new audience. They hovered around the access door at the tube's base that Aral had seen earlier. They chatted for a moment, some pointing at the tube, some listening with their hands on their hips or folded behind their back. They then turned to a large toolbox lying on the ground. One of the men kneeled and opened it. Aral saw him hand something to one of the others, while he pulled out a large battery-powered circular saw. He laid the saw on the ground and pulled out a transparent face mask. He put the mask on, picked up the saw, and stepped back to the tube. He placed the inert blade against the tube, just outside of the door's frame. He gripped the tool with both hands. But before activating it, he looked over his shoulder at Brondl, who'd worked his way up to the front.

"Ready?" the spotter asked.

"Go ahead," Brondl said.

With a burst of sparks and an earsplitting scream, the saw spat to life. The spotter pushed inward, causing the blade to penetrate the metal. Even though he was illuminated by the others' lights, the shower of orange sparks lit up the entire site like a bonfire. As he pushed the blade upward to follow the outline of the door, he squinted against the sparks, which bounced off his face mask. Aral wondered what damage the sparks might've done had he not been wearing the mask, as surely there were bits of metal mixed in with the sparks.

Aral covered her ears. The sawing metal was almost as loud as the airship's engine she'd heard that morning. But there was something skull-rattling about this sound—something the airship hadn't done. Now it seemed that the saw's shrill scream would shake her teeth from her skull. Tears welled up in her eyes. She pushed her fingers harder into her ears to keep the sound out.

The sawing was slow going. Several minutes

must've passed and the spotter had only worked the tool three feet up the side of the tube.

And then Aral noticed something. Aside from the torrent of sparks, the spotter's uniform seemed to be blowing and snapping in the wind, as if a powerful gust of air were pushing out of the tube through the breach he'd made. From where she stood, Aral could feel nothing—not even one of the soft breezes she'd come to expect in the Cthonian desert, especially at night as the air cooled. Perhaps she was imagining it. Perhaps the spotter's clothing was only blowing because of the sparks.

When the spotter finally reached the end of the outline, the door blew outward. As if someone had placed a bomb behind it, the door popped out against the spotter, knocking him on his back and sending the still-whirring saw into the sand two yards away. The square slab of metal thumped lifeless to the ground, but the sand around the newly made door whipped and swirled as a thick, hot column of air exploded outward. The spotters gathered around the tube stepped back and shielded their eyes against what felt like a giant wind tunnel blowing miles and miles of stuffy, stale air straight at them.

Covering her eyes with her right hand, Aral stepped to the side until she was no longer in the direct line of the blast. When the wind around her died down, she uncovered her eyes and looked at the tube.

By now all of the spotters had stepped aside. Billows of sand still raged at the hole that had just been cut in the twenty-yard-wide pipe. Still, Aral had the impression the wind was slowing somewhat. What was happening? She let her eyes drift upward in the dark, trying to follow the tube up into the clouds, which churned somewhere up above, but because of the after-midnight darkness, she couldn't tell. And then she realized the wind must've been the result of the air pressure inside the tube being different from the air pressure outside. In the same way a punctured tire hisses out a gush of air until the tire is flat, the tube was letting out a much larger volume of compressed atmosphere.

As the intensity of the airstream died, Aral felt certain this was what had happened. Many minutes passed before the spotters could approach the tube. When only a small breeze trickled out, a team of spotters stepped up and peered into the black rectangle that leered at them in the dark.

"Careful," Brondl said, stepping up. "One step at a time."

The spotter in front nodded. He adjusted his headlamp and placed his right hand on the side of the hole. He gave Brondl and the others a thumbs-up and eased his head and shoulders into the darkness.

From where she stood, Aral couldn't see anything inside the tube aside from the circle of white light that danced from the spotter's headlamp. The interior of the tube was pitch-black. Inch by inch, the spotter worked his way in, disappearing from view. The black hole now gaped at the team, expressionless, with only a flash of white light now and then as the spotter must've been looking around inside.

"It's okay!" he shouted. His voice echoed up the length of the tube. Aral sighed and relaxed her shoulders. She looked around. The others were visibly relieved. Brondl ran his hand over the back of his neck, massaging his muscles. He looked to the remaining members of the team that had examined the tube and cut the hole and motioned for them to step up to the door.

One by one, they walked up and stepped in. They moved more surely than the first man had, now that he had entered safely and called to them.

With the spotters inside, Brondl stepped up and peeked in. Tell nudged Aral forward.

"Go on," he whispered. "Don't you wanna see? Look." He pointed. Several other spotters who'd been watching were stepping up to the hole.

Aral turned and glanced at her team leader. Her eyes twinkled in the dark. "Can we?"

"Go ahead. I'm with you."

The two stepped up and paused just outside the door. They waited as several others took turns stepping in, looking around, and coming out. Aral glanced at the sheet of metal that had been cut from the pipe. Because the tube was twenty yards in diameter, the sheet curved slightly, looking like a four-by-six-foot sled, the still-closed door anchored in the center. Aral tapped the metal with her foot and marveled when the entire sheet slid several inches in the sand.

"Aral," Tell said, tapping her on the shoulder. "Come on."

It was their turn. They stepped in.

The first thing that struck Aral about the interior of the tube was that there was no wind, unlike the blinding gale that had first been unleashed. That, and the temperature inside was at least ten degrees higher than the outside. *Strange*, she thought, looking at the super-thin edges of the door, *it doesn't look insulated*. They were now completely encased in that ultralight metal, with only the four-by-six-foot hole connecting them to the outside world.

Beyond the temperature, the sound quality inside was different. First of all, the rumble of the water rushing up a second internal tube was amplified in what reminded Aral of the sound of the airship's engines, only not as earsplitting. Beyond that, Aral clearly had the sense of being closed in, locked off, suffocated even. Every move, every breath, every sound that Brondl, the team, Tell, or she made was amplified tenfold, with the rumble of the water blanketing them all.

Aral looked around, her vision circumscribed by the small white circle cast by her headlamp. As she did, the others milled about, looking up, down, left, right, and chatting with each other about how to proceed with the plan to climb the tube. But Aral ignored them. She was lost in the wonder of discovery.

The floor was just sand—like a colossal hypodermic needle, the twenty-yard-diameter pipe planted itself straight into the ground as if burrowing through the planet itself. And most of the interior was sand, because there were only two structures inside the tube. Just inches from where the team had cut the door, a metal ladder was affixed to the wall. The ladder stretched up, up, up . . . all the way up to Ætheria. The spotters huddled around its base and were talking with animated gestures to each other and to Brondl, who scrutinized the ladder with tight-lipped determination.

Directly opposite the ladder, a network of smaller yet nonetheless massive pipes burst forth from the ground and climbed the length of the pipe. There were three. The largest was two to three yards in diameter and seemed affixed to the side of the larger pipe, like the spine of a whale in illustrated children's books. *That must be the water*, Aral thought. She scanned the base of the water tube, but saw no signs of seepage. *It must be very well made—completely watertight.* The other two pipes—themselves attached to the water pipe—were only two or three feet in diameter. *Those must transport the cthoneum gas and carbon dioxide*, she thought. She stepped up to the cluster and placed her hand on one of the smaller pipes. The metal was cool—not cold—to her touch. Aside from that, she felt no vibrations, no rumble . . . no sign that anything was being extracted from the ground.

She removed her hand and stepped to the middle of the tube. She looked up. She gasped. The view was awe-inspiring. If she had not been looking straight up, she could have just as well been looking into a never-ending tunnel. The pipes, the ladder, and the walls of the tube itself stretched up and up and up until Aral's headlamp weakened and she could see only a hazy, fading circle of dark—a circle of dark that led straight to Ætheria. For a brief instant, she wondered what Ætherians would see if they were to look down the pipe from above? What had Máire seen those sixteen years ago when she'd come down? An endless tunnel leading into dark? Aral wondered if Ætherians might be looking down right now . . .

"Okay, okay, okay, okay, okay, okay," Brondl's

echoing voice stirred her from her daydream. She looked over at the commander. His expression seemed more relaxed—satisfied, even. "Let's clear out and let our team go to work. If you're not in the climbing team, you're dismissed."

SEVEN

"**T**HEY'RE AT THE CLOUD." TELL'S VOICE drifted into Aral's flailing dreams. She blinked her eyes and looked around. The tent had begun to glow yellowish in the early morning light. She sat up. Some of the bunks around her were empty, but a few other spotters were stirring and sitting up. A few bunks still contained sleeping spotters. Aral didn't feel rested. She had tossed throughout the few hours she'd had to sleep. The excitement of what lay ahead worked stronger than caffeine.

"What time is it?" she asked with a yawn.

"Just after seven. Boy, you were out. You need

to get up and get to work!" He turned to the others and shouted, "Come on! Let's go! We've got water to get to!"

Aral turned to the side and planted her feet on the floor. She blinked up at Tell, who stood.

"Seven . . . wait, what did you say? About the team?"

"We think they're in the cloud," Tell repeated, his voice more urgent.

Aral looked around again, as if trying to make sense of his words. She stood and pulled on her utility vest, which she had laid on her footlocker the night before.

"The cloud? You're sure? How do you know?"

"We stopped receiving their transmissions at about six. The only explanation is that the radio isn't transmitting through that cloud."

"Are they alright?" Aral stood, adrenaline fully waking her. "What are we going to do?"

"What *you* are going to do is get outside and help with the drilling. But you can come see, first."

Tell pulled Aral from her dormitory tent to the command center tables. She saw four or five spotters leaning over the table. They were poring over maps, charts, and printouts while Brondl sat at one end of the table, both of his hands gripping a headset that was connected to a radio receiver box that glittered with a constellation of red, white, and green lights. To the immediate right of the radio, a teletex machine spat out a sheet of paper inches at a time. As she approached, she saw that the paper contained lines of text.

"Look," Tell said, leading Aral around to Brondl's side. Brondl nodded at the two and continued listening. His face was intent. Tell sat Aral down and reached over to a small stack of paper next to the teletex. He slid the top sheets over to Aral and planted them directly in front of her.

"Read."

"What is this?"

"Whenever one of the spotters radios in, their words are transcribed—both on microfile and in hard copy. This is what they've reported so far, along with the times of their transmissions."

Aral turned to the table and scooted in. She leaned forward, wiped sleep from her eyes, ran her tongue over teeth that felt fuzzy, and read.

TIME 0021/HR 76/VO2 35 ml/kg/min The entire team is in the tube. Heading up now.

TIME 0510/HR 112/VO2 35 ml/kg/min Slow going. We are all exhausted. We must be at about two or three miles up by now. We're putting on our masks—the air is getting thin. No changes to report.

TIME 0547/HR 110/VO2 35 ml/kg/min Something's changing. We think we've reached the level of the cloud, but not sure. The temperature has spiked, and we can feel an electric current in the air. There's thunder on the other side of the tube. The ambient electricity is interfering with our radios, monitors, and oxygen regulators. Up above there are some kind of long metal spikes pointing

down. We should be able to get through,
though, as long as

Aral looked up. "Where's the next sheet?" she
asked. "What's happened?"

Tell shrugged his shoulders. "That's just it. There
isn't one. What you're seeing is the last transmission
we received. The signal cut mid-sentence. That's why
we think they're in the cloud. Brondl has been glued
to the radio ever since, but we've heard nothing.
Nothing. Even the homing signals on the ComPods
have gone silent. Until the transmission cut, we were
able to follow their ascent, altitude, and vital stats.
Look," he said, lifting his head to indicate two men
to Brondl's right. They sat hunched over a glowing
screen overlaid with concentric orange circles.

"They're keeping their eye on the homing beacons
inside the ComPods. They *should* be showing up on
that screen, but just after the last transmission, the
screen went blank."

"But wait." Aral glanced at Brondl. Sleepy bags
clung beneath his eyes. He'd clearly been up all night.

She looked back at the sheet, her heart rate quickening. "0547. That was an hour and half ago. You mean there's been radio silence since? And no sign of the ComPods?"

Tell nodded and frowned.

"That's right. Last we knew they were just below fifteen thousand feet—probably just above the cloud, I imagine."

Before Tell could finish his sentence, Aral spun around and dashed out of the tent. She heard his footsteps behind her. She ran thirty or forty yards from the tent's entrance and looked east.

The sun, though perpetually hidden behind the ever-present, yellowish cloud above, had by now come fully up and warmed the desert to a sweltering heat. A thin layer of sweat emerged almost instantly over her forehead, face, and neck. Thirty yards away, a group of spotters milled around some heavy machinery they'd removed from the airship. They were installing the apparatus at the spot where Aral's hydrosensor had detected the water. They were making the preparations to begin drilling.

A little more than twenty yards away, the dark gray, uninterrupted form of the tube sat stolid, unperturbed, like some sort of monument or massive memorial built centuries before. She looked at the tube's base and could make out a dark hole on the tube's left side. *The portal*, she thought. The sand just outside the hole wafted and swirled, blown about by a powerful stream of air pushing out from inside the tube.

She followed the tube up, trying to imagine where the team might be. As she had seen before, the tube stretched up, up, up in the distance, disappearing into the cloud.

———

A day passed with no news.

An acid rainstorm battered the team, the tents, and the parked airship, forcing the guards and the rest of the spotters to stay inside. The tents protected against the acid, but on bare skin it would cause irritation within hours.

Clearly worried, Brondl had an unending supply of tasks to keep the spotters who weren't drilling busy: anchoring the tents, preparing food, feeding and watering the eqūs who remained tethered to the guy wires, taking the eqūs on short patrols, cleaning, making beds, rearranging the command post, filing reports, drilling, making plans for a potential rescue operation, communicating with the CCC, and cleaning the latrines behind the tent. He also ordered the construction of a collapsible passage to connect the tent to the tube—"So we can access the tube no matter what the weather is," he said.

Aside from those involved in planning a rescue, no one talked about what might have happened with the reconnaissance team. Everyone knew that they were highly trained. But no one had ever had to deal with anything like this before.

Several hours after darkness fell, panic erupted.

Aral had just finished cleaning up after a day of keeping the well drill dry when one of the spotters back at the command center tables began shouting.

"Look! Two of the pods! They're back! I've got a signal! Brondl! Everyone!"

A surge of adrenaline coursed through Aral's body. She bounded to the tables, where dozens of the others had already poured in. They were crowding around one of the computer screens.

"Lemme through! Lemme through!" Brondl had heard the spotter's voice from the transit tunnel and pushed his way through the growing crowd. He strode up to the computer screen and the technician who'd shouted, while others elbowed their way closer to the tables, each spotter trying to stand on their toes to see what was happening. From her spot, Aral could see two dots flashing at intervals of three seconds in the top right-hand portion of the screen. She couldn't tell what she was seeing, but as soon as Brondl stepped up, the technician gestured and spoke wildly, his throat veins strained from the effort and his face red with emotion. Brondl nodded and sat, picking up the radio headphones and putting them on.

"Quiet!!" Brondl screamed, his eyes bulging. The rattled din instantly ceased, and everyone tried not to make a sound as Brondl listened and stared at the blips on the screen.

Hardly thirty seconds had passed when Brondl yanked the headphones from his ears and stood, grumbling. He scanned the room and his eyes settled on Tell, who stood across the tables from Aral.

"Tell, I want you to get your team ready in ten minutes. To leave. The pods have landed about a mile from here," he looked down and tapped the screen, "north by northwest. That's what we're seeing on the screen: it's the pods' homing beacon. They've fallen back to the ground. I can hear nothing via radio. But we need to recover those pods." He straightened up and concluded with, "They've been ejected. For what reason, we can't tell. Only the pods themselves can tell us any more about where their bearers are . . . or what may have happened to them."

At Brondl's order, Aral burst into movement. She hurtled back to her bunk and pulled on her utility pants and vest, clipped her headlamp to her head, and attached a full canteen to both sides of her belt. With gear shaking and clanking, she ran back to the tent's entrance, where Tell was speaking in a low voice with Brondl. The commander clutched some sort of electronic device in his hand just bigger than a handheld radio transmitter. Aral saw that this was a hand-held homing scanner designed to lead them to the fallen ComPods. As Brondl was explaining something to Tell in clipped, rapid-fire sentences, he looked up between words and pointed out across the desert before bringing his hand down again and pointing at the scanner screen. He was explaining which way the team would head.

When Brondl had finished, Tell looked up and nodded to Aral.

"Ready?" he asked.

"Ready," she said, returning his nod.

Tell placed his hand on her shoulder. "Good. Ah, there's Estrella and the others. C'mon, let's go out."

Aral turned to her right and smiled a tight-lipped grin at her friend. Within a minute, the other team members were assembled just outside the tent door, each busy tightening their gear belts and adjusting their headlamps.

Darkness had engulfed Cthonia, but at least the rain had stopped, allowing them to move about unprotected.

"Okay," Tell began, directing everyone into a small huddle. "Here's the plan. According to the homing scanner, the pods have landed 4,572 feet that way, so just less than a mile. We'll take our eqūs to move faster, but once we get to within fifty yards or so, we'll need to walk." He looked in the direction of the now invisible, broiling cloud above. "Once we're on our eqūs, we'll need our lights. In the day, the pods would stand out well enough, what with their being shiny black and all, but at night . . . well, we've got the scanner and our headlamps. Between the ten of us, we'll find them."

He looked the team over. "Questions?"

Everyone on the team shook their heads.

"Good. Well, let's go find these things."

Though Aral had been glad over the past day to have a rest from riding, she was happy to mount Ferda again. When she rounded the tent to where the ten animals stood harnessed to guy wires, the eqūs opened her eyes wide and whinnied a hello through the dusk. The others' eqūs echoed Ferda's cry when they too saw their riders trotting in behind Aral.

"Okay, girl, here we go," she said in a comforting tone. She reached up and clicked on her headlamp, which cast its bright light over the eqūs's shiny brown body and leather reins. She worked her way up the tether and untied the animal. She led her several steps away to a spot that seemed clear of any guy wires. She reached up, grabbed the pommel, and launched herself into the saddle. Ferda shook her head and nickered. Aral gave her a few light taps with her heels, turning the animal around until she spotted Tell on his eqūs.

Tell was already working his way northeast.

"Okay, everyone move easy until we get through these wires," he shouted back.

"Got it," Aral said, echoed by Estrella and a few others behind her.

The team worked its way snake-like through the matrix of nearly invisible guy wires. Aral kept her eyes forward, ducking and weaving as the wires swept in from the dark, like spectral, linear forms that materialized only seconds before colliding with the rider. Following her lead, Ferda marched along softly, gingerly, as if the eqūs were aware she could not go any faster here without risking a nasty fall.

Up ahead, Tell sat upright but with his head alternating between looking ahead for surprise guy wires and looking down at his scanner. The black silhouette of his body blocked the device's light from view, but Aral knew Tell was following its lead. And she was following his.

After a few minutes of this bobbing-and-weaving style of riding, the team pulled clear of the guy wires, which suddenly vanished behind them, leaving only black and Tell's eerie silhouette ahead.

"A half mile," he said over his shoulder, seemingly just loud enough for only Aral to hear. She nodded, even though she knew he couldn't see her. Tell turned forward and spurred his eqūs, who sped to a trot. Aral followed suit. She squeezed her thighs against the animal and lifted her rear from the bouncing saddle. Even though she knew they were through the wires, she couldn't help but duck and grunt with the expectation that at any moment one would spring from the dark and whip her across the face. If not for this fear, she probably would've enjoyed the nighttime trot. Night was always her favorite time to ride. Then she could close her eyes and depend on the eqūs's eyes to guide her around the rolling, sandy dunes surrounding the CCC. In moments such as those, she felt that she was flying—soaring, even—high above the desert landscape that her people, the Cthonians, had settled hundreds of years before.

But now she kept her eyes open and alert. Now was no time for games.

About ten minutes had passed when Tell reined his eqūs in, slowing to a walk and then stopping. He turned the animal around to face the oncoming team. They filed into place with snorts and tramping hooves.

"From here we go on foot," he said as he turned the scanner around for the team to see the screen. Aral peered through the dark, but could only make out an orangish grid flanked by some numbers and a small dot flashing toward the middle of the screen. "According to this," Tell continued, turning the device back around, "we are within fifty yards. So we need to dismount and spread out at ten-yard intervals in standard arrow-first search formation. No one walks faster than heel-and-toe with a *full* lateral sweep of your headlamps. Got it?"

A chorus of *yes*'s answered.

"Good. You'll need to walk your equs with you, because," he looked around, his white headlamp casting a fast-moving white circle over rocks, shrubs, and stubby cacti, "I don't see anywhere we could tie them." He faced the others but tried to angle his head so he did not blind them with his light. "Keep your eyes open. These things are made to withstand anything—theoretically, at least—so they should be intact. Let's go!"

The team spread out. Aral worked her way over to Tell's right. He gestured to the others to spread out on either side of him, leaving him as the apex of the search formation: a long, baseless triangle of spotters spread out like a migrating flock of geese inching their way across the valley. Once in position, she didn't wait for any sign from Tell to move forward. *Step, step, step, step*—she placed her feet one after the other, making sure to keep her advancing heel in line with the toe of her other foot. With each step, she paused and rotated her head a full one hundred and eighty degrees, so that she—along with the others on either side of her—would leave no square inch of Cthonian soil unsearched.

With each step, Aral felt her breathing become quicker and quicker. In her right hand, Ferda's rein began to slip through her sweaty palm. She shifted the tether from one hand to the other. Behind her, Ferda let out a snort as if to ask what was wrong. She took a deep breath and whispered, more to calm herself that to calm the eqūs.

"It's okay, girl, don't worry . . . "

In the beam of her light, only the irregular and dancing forms of a desert fully empty of water met her gaze. Sand, pebbles, rocks, some decaying twigs, and a few browning cacti—nothing more. Beyond the light, darkness. Her breath came in gasps, and fear began to take hold. While her mind told her nothing could be out here, she couldn't help imagining what might be slinking around in the black, just beyond the reach of her light. Some animal that had gone unnoticed by the Cthonians? A predator? Or maybe a group of Ætherians that had come down and were creeping around Cthonia? At the thought of Ætheria, her heart knocked against her ribs. How many of them could there be? Would they be like Máire? Aral recalled Máire's lessons in class of the Ætherians all being dark and much shorter than the Cthonians—both effects of living for so long in such harsh conditions, constantly exposed to intense ultraviolet radiation from the sun. Aside from their physical difference, Máire had also always said that the Cthonians and the Ætherians were not so different. They both wanted to survive in harsh conditions. They both tried to maintain a normal existence after the rest of the Cthonian population had died out. And there were even people in Ætheria that dreamed of one day returning to Cthonia . . .

Aral froze.

Something up ahead and to the right caught her eye. Something different—a movement? A shimmer?

She shot a look ahead and to her left—to Tell, who was still moving forward ten yards ahead. His feet continued their inch-by-inch advance. He'd seen nothing.

Aral looked again in the direction of the movement. She scanned her head, allowing the light from her headlamp to bathe the night with white light. Nothing. The same pale desert as before.

And then an explosion of terror shot through her. She saw it again.

About fifteen yards ahead of her and just to the right, a twinkle pierced through the dark like a pair of predator's eyes. She took a full step, this time in the direction of the glint. There could be no doubt: it flashed again from behind a tuft of scrub. Was it an animal hiding from her? Whatever it was, it was small enough to hide behind a sickly plant.

Reassured that whatever it was, it wasn't large enough to be a creeping Ætherian, she took several more full steps forward, keeping her light trained on the thing. For the first time since she dismounted and started walking, she was aware of the sound of her footsteps, which seemed thunderous in the tense silence.

Another glimmer. And this time, she saw another, about twenty or thirty yards away from the first, glinting at her through the dark.

Aral took a deep breath and walked forward until . . .

"Tell! Here they are!"

Aral kneeled before the first pod, which lay like a sleeping fawn behind a patch of scrub. With her headlamp pointed at it, the pod shimmered and glistened. Brondl had shown them one a few days before, but she didn't remember it being so shiny. At first glance, she marveled at how pristine the pod appeared. If it had plummeted twenty-five thousand feet or more and landed here, it would've been hurtling down at nearly four hundred miles per hour. Yet she could not see a scratch or dent. She glanced around for a crater—some site of impact—but saw nothing. Only more sand and pebbles.

She leaned in. Behind her, eighteen feet pounded their way toward her.

"The other one's over there!" she shouted, pointing at the second glimmer. Several of the spotters trampled in the direction of the pod, the white circles of light from their headlamps dancing over the sand.

Aral's body pulsed with adrenaline—at the find, at what this could mean for the Cthonians' water, at what secrets the pods contained. She looked at the pod. As before, the mass of wires and tubes sprouted from one end. But something was different—strange. She reached forward and ran her hand under the tangled mass of wire, lifting them a few inches for a better look. No, she hadn't imagined it. They looked as though they had been ripped out. Their ends were flayed, torn, and garbled with a mess of wiry strands of copper that reached out like hundreds of dead spider legs.

"Is it intact?" Tell said, sliding to a stop over Aral's left shoulder. He was breathing as hard as if he had just run a race.

"Yes," she said, placing her hand on the pod. It felt cold. She rolled it over to where she knew the ridged patches to be.

"We've got it!" one of the other spotters shouted from the direction of the other pod. "But it's all smashed in. It looks like it landed straight on a boulder!"

"C'mon," Tell said. "Let's get these back to Brondl. Now."

EIGHT

FORTY SPOTTERS CLAMORED AND PUSHED TO get a glimpse of what was happening at the command post tables. Because she had first seen the pods, Aral was allowed a spot next to Brondl. Tell stood to her left, followed by Estrella and the rest of Tell's team. As for Brondl, he had turned the two pods over to his technicians, who worked with screwdrivers to open the devices. In the light of the tent, Aral saw that, while the first pod seemed relatively undamaged, the second was battered and misshapen from smacking into a boulder at four hundred miles per hour. While the technicians worked, Brondl stood iron-jawed, his arms folded across his chest, watching.

Amid the bedlam, the technicians first focused on working their tools into the ridged latches and twisting the undamaged pod's receded bolts. They worked simultaneously—one opened one end latch; the other, the other. With one latch left, a technician held the pod in place with both hands, while the other worked at the remaining lock.

With a crack, the pod opened. The spotters fell silent. One technician peeled one half of the pod back like the half of a ball sliced in two. The other reached in and extracted a microchip from an array of wires, transistor plates, and flashing lights. He passed the chip to his colleague, who inserted it into a Common Sequential Convey port on the side of the teletex printer. With the chip in place, he ran his fingers across the teletex screen and navigated through a series of menus. He pressed the screen one last time, and the teletex began printing.

They then repeated the process with the second

pod. Because of the damage to its shell, however, the technicians could not get the screws to turn and had to resort to hammering screwdrivers into the pod's seam to wedge it open.

"Careful," Brondl said, his eyes on the team. "We don't want to break what's inside. Assuming, of course, it's not already smashed."

The technicians didn't respond. With sweat glistening on their faces, they twisted and turned their tools into the sides of the mangled pod. After several minutes of inserting their screwdrivers, straining, removing the tools, reinserting them, and prying again, they wedged the two halves of the pod apart.

"Dammit," Brondl said when they exposed the insides. Aral stood on her toes for a clear look.

Whereas the first pod had been entirely intact and functioning, the interior of the second revealed a jumble of loose transistor parts and deracinated wires. It looked more like a toolbox containing the parts of some electronic device rather than a working monitor and transponder.

"Do you think you can get the chip?" Brondl asked.

One of the technicians leaned in and shone a small flashlight into the chip's port. He reached over with a pair of needle-nose pliers and worked the chip out. He stood up straight and held the data-holding device out to Brondl. It was warped in the middle.

"I can try," he said in a deflated voice, turning the chip over for Brondl to inspect it from every angle. "You check the printout, and I'll see what I can do"

Though the tent had been noisy since the spotters put it up, each member of the forty-person group could now hear every shift, hum, and zip as the printer finished eking out page after page of printouts.

"These should give us a good deal of information," the other technician said. "We should get a decent picture of what happened."

The technician handed the sheets to Brondl, who read the pages with one hand while he stroked his chin with his other. Aral kept her eyes on the commander for any sign—any emotion that could reveal what he was learning. She had become oblivious to the others as her gaze melted into watching Brondl's dark eyes, which grew ever darker as they read.

He turned the page, shifting the top page to the rear. He read, expressionless.

Midway through the third page, his countenance fell. His eyebrows crumpled and the corners of his mouth inched their way downward. His face grew red.

He turned the page. By now a film of sweat had appeared on his forehead. The muscles in his jaw tensed. He looked up, at the same time lowering the pages to stomach level. Aral heard their flutter as his hand dropped.

Speechless, Brondl let his eyes wander aimlessly around the room. He seemed to be looking at everyone, while at the same time seeing no one. He said nothing, but Aral could feel his anger mounting. Like a volcano whose pressure grew and grew, until finally . . .

"How can this be happening?!" he spouted,

slamming the pages onto the table nearest him with a smack.

At his eruption, the spotters nearest him let out an audible gasp. Some stepped back from the table.

"Sir," Tell ventured in a meek voice. "Sir, what is it?"

"They're killers," Brondl muttered, avoiding Tell's and everyone else's gaze. "Those Ætherians . . . they're . . . *murderers*." He stepped back from the table.

"Sir?"

"Williams," Brondl said to the technician who'd handed him the printout.

"Yes?"

"Print enough copies of this for everyone. I'm going to radio in." He turned to the first technician, who was now peering through a magnifying glass at the bent data chip from the damaged pod. "Is it going to work?" Brondl asked.

The technician shook his head. "Don't count on it. In any case, I don't have the tools here to try and salvage what might be left. I just don't get it. Those pods were supposed to withstand anything. But I guess we never figured it would hit a rock at more than four hundred miles per hour. That's enough force to shatter anything." He sat up and ran his hand over the back of his neck. "I guess . . . "

Brondl glanced around at the others. He took one final glance at the papers in his hand and crumpled them into a ball. "I'm going to need some time alone," he fumed.

For the first time since he read the report, he paused and looked around the tent, glaring each of the spotters in the eye. When his eyes rested on Aral's, she couldn't hold his gaze. She lowered her eyes.

"But first, all of you," Brondl said in a commanding voice. He seemed to have regained his composure since the initial shock. "If this is accurate, then the Ætherians have killed not one, but several of our spotters. Let's just hope that my son . . . " His voice trailed off. He took a deep breath as if trying to calm himself and let out a long, exasperated sigh. "So much for peace.

"I'm going to radio the CCC and tell them what happened. I'm going to ask for their direction, but," he looked Aral straight in the eye, as if trying to let her know that he saw her look away, "if they've attacked us, there will be consequences. *That* I can assure you."

———

When the copies had finished printing, Aral scooped up a set with trembling hands and went to her dormitory tent to read. The other spotters spread themselves around their tents to do the same—some sat or lay on their bunks, some paced back and forth, some walked outside and read by the light of their headlamps. A panicked, nervous energy filled the air. Brondl's tone had been terrifying, but he'd not said enough for anyone to make sense of what was happening. As the spotters read, Brondl left the tent altogether. No one spoke to him as he stormed out. His face showed that he didn't want to talk to anyone.

Enough ambient light from the control center LEDs allowed Aral to read without her headlamp. Flipping through the three sheets, she noticed a printout similar to the one Tell had shown her earlier, the only difference being that this one contained heart rate and blood oxygen saturation statistics, along with the time of transmission and recording of the wearer's words. Aral looked at the first page header:

Mira Babel. 18 years old. Female. Cthonian Spotter Second Tier.

Hmm, she thought. *Eighteen. Two years older than me.* She tried to remember which of the six in the team this was. But since she had never really known any of the spotters, she couldn't place Mira's face. The printout said nothing about her height, weight, hair color, or anything else to clue her in to who she was. She could've been anybody.

Aral skimmed over the papers and found where the printout resumed from the previous entry she'd read, before contact was lost. It began at 10:23 in the morning—about five hours since the last transmission. Seeing this, Aral could conclude that either the climb had been uneventful during that time, or that there had been some problem with their equipment that incapacitated the recorder. Aral read:

TIME 1023/HR 112/VO2 35 ml/kg/min Static electricity and temperature both rising. Can you hear me? Hello? The temperature here must be twenty degrees warmer than the rest of the tube. We must be entering the cloud. The temperature is causing the team to slow down. Sweating uncontrollably. The higher we go, the more and more sparks I can see around the sides of the tube. There are little spikes—like little lightning rods—all around the tube that must be there to discharge electricity. I've never felt anything like it.

TIME 1101/HR 114/VO2 34 ml/kg/min Every few minutes, there is a big discharge. It hurts. I see sparks jumping from the others' hands, feet, or bodies to the metal ladder or sides. The noise outside is growing. Like some kind of animal or storm beating into the tube from the outside. Maybe thunder?

TIME 1200/HR 110/VO2 32 ml/kg/min We're screaming over the storm. The shocks are too much. We're stuck in some kind of spikes pointing downward. Like this whole thing is a trap to keep us down. Can't be sure, though. We're going to have to unharness and free climb to get through. See some platforms up ahead. For maintenance? Looks like we should be able to stand.

TIME 1533/HR 112/VO2 32 ml/kg/min Taylar is stuck. We can't reach him. His pod and mask are wedged in the spikes. Lenóre is hanging back to help. I am going to push forward. With no harness.

TIME 1611/HR 122/VO2 29 ml/kg/min Stan slipped and fell. I can't see him, but it's because we had to take off our harnesses. I've tried shouting down to Lenóre, who is helping Taylar, but I'm not getting any answer. I don't think our radios are transmitting at all. The remaining three of us are pushing up.

TIME 1703/HR 125/VO2 27 ml/kg/min I've made it through the first set of spikes, but there are others. I've already slipped twice but have been able to catch myself. Who put these spikes here? Why? The noise outside is so loud, I can't even hear my hands and feet climbing around. If I get shocked one more time, I may have to turn back—it's every few seconds now.

TIME 1719/HR 120/VO2 22 ml/kg/min We must [inaudible], now. The noise has calmed down, and the electricity is fading. There are two ladders now—one on either side of the water tube and the other pipes. We're standing on a [inaudible]. We're hooking in and continuing.

TIME 1749/HR 138/VO2 21 ml/kg/min We have to [inaudible]. I can hardly feel my [inaudible]. And now it's getting harder and harder to breathe, despite our masks.

The electrical storm fried all of my instruments: my respirator, my altimeter, my radio, my watch, even. I am hoping that the pod [inaudible].

TIME 1755/HR 140/VO2 19 ml/kg/min We've gone from extremely hot in the cloud to extremely cold. The temperature is plummeting.

TIME 1834/HR 142/VO2 18 ml/kg/min So cold. So cold. Not feeling my fingers or face. I have to move my [inaudible].

TIME 1835/HR 151/VO2 17 ml/kg/min Still climbing.

TIME 2001/HR 160/VO2 17 ml/kg/min Errie is about to pass out. Can't tell why. Lack of oxygen? Cold? Fatigue?

TIME 2121/HR 156/VO2 16 ml/kg/min Something's up above. Some kind of [inaudible]. Is this the end?

TIME 2123/HR 130/VO2 16 ml/kg/min Door's locked. [inaudible] is working to get it open while I keep my [inaudible]. It looks like this door hasn't been opened in a while. Work is going slow. We feel like we're moving in slow motion. So hard to breathe. And so cold.

TIME 2155/HR 136/VO2 16 ml/kg/min We got the door open and are [inaudible]. Heading out now.

TIME 2209/HR 162/VO2 15 ml/kg/min We're up top. Above the clouds. I can't believe what we're seeing—it's like we've landed on some other planet. We are on some sort of [inaudible]. There's another about two hundred yards away, and from here I can see [inaudible]. It is difficult to [inaudible], and we can't even [inaudible]. The wind is strong—maybe fifty or sixty miles per hour. And it's constant—not in gusts. The cold is unbearable. It's just Jackson and me out. Errie is back in the tube. I think she's unconscious. This place is [inaudible]. We're going to try and move if we can. We have to hurry.

TIME 2211/HR 167/VO2 14 ml/kg/min We've

split up. I've made it about fifty feet away from the hatch. Jackson went around to the other side. There is a compact building on the island that has part of it hanging off. I can see the big tube from below. It comes into this building. This is the power generator and water purification plant, just like Máire said. The other islands all have buildings on them, too. It reminds me of some kind of [inaudible] tubes and rounded buildings. No life sighted yet.

TIME 2214/HR 140/VO2 15 ml/kg/ min Hypoxia and frostbite. I can hardly stay [inaudible]. I have no more feeling in [inaudible]. We should've stayed together.

TIME 2215/HR 98/VO2 15 ml/kg/min So cold. Can't breathe. My vision is [inaudible]. Can't think straight anymore. Feel like I am sleeping and walking and floating.

TIME 2216/HR 143/VO2 13 ml/kg/ min Jackson's screaming. That they will get us, kill us, that they know who

[inaudible]. They are going to kill
[inaudible].

TIME 2217/HR 178/VO2 13 ml/kg/min No time
to lose. Attack before they do. Over.

**TIME 2217/HR 30/VO2 12 ml/kg/
min** Aaaaahhhhh! Help us!

Before Aral had finished reading, the tent was
churning with gasps, curses, and heated discussion.

"What's Brondl going to do?"

"It's the Ætherians!"

"What happened to the others?"

"Are they still in that tube?"

"How many of those people—those *things*—are up
there?"

"They've killed our spotters, and now they're going
to kill us all!"

"They're not people. They're animals.
Those . . . parasites, is what they are! Parasites that are
sucking us dry! That's *our* water they're sucking up!"

Aral's thoughts swirled. *How could they make such*

certain claims? What did they know? Feeling her face grow hot, she crumpled the sheets into a ball that she threw onto the floor. She stood and stormed out of her dormitory tent and into the command center area. About ten or twenty spotters had pulled up seats and were arguing at the tops of their voices. They seemed to be screaming over each other all at once. At the head of the nine tables, the two technicians were fooling with the radio, the teletex, and the homing sensor for any other pods that may have fallen. Aral had the impression that all they were doing was trying to hide behind their headphones and technology from the screaming that was filling the entire tent. Amid the myriad voices, Aral felt her temples throbbing and her eyes watering. She scanned the gathering area until she spotted Estrella, who was in a heated discussion with one of the other girls. Aral worked her way through the mob of spotters, grabbed her friend by the sleeve, and pulled her through the tent's door and outside.

The night air provided a refreshing respite from

the stuffy tent air. As the two moved to about twenty or thirty feet from the door, Aral glanced upward, imagining what the team members up there might have seen.

"Can you believe it?" Aral asked Estrella once the two were out of earshot.

"Honestly? No. No, I can't."

"But it's there. They're up there," Aral nodded skyward. "I can't believe this is happening."

"What's he going to do? Brondl, I mean . . . " Estrella glanced around to make sure that they were not being listened to. All around the tent darkness throbbed. The only other people outside were the tent's guards and a few other spotters who had spread out in the sand in front of the tent and were having similar discussions.

"Let's just hope they're alright," Aral said. "Do you think he'll send more people up? A rescue team, maybe?"

"I have no idea. Are there rules for this?"

"Dunno," Aral looked down, her eyes cloudy with thought. "Doesn't it seem strange?"

"What do you mean?"

"I mean," Aral turned and glanced back at the tent, which was now behind her. Estrella faced the tent, and Aral stood between the two. "What we don't know. What happened up there? To Stan and Errie? That's just one ComPod transcript. And it's incomplete. We don't know anything, really. Where are the other ComPods? Why didn't they eject? They haven't seen *anything* else on the homing screen. When will . . . "

Estrella lifted her hand to silence her friend. She nodded subtly and looked behind over Aral's right shoulder. Estrella puckered her lips as if to say *shhhh*. She widened her eyes. *Look behind you.*

Aral turned. From the soupy darkness, Brondl marched back into the tent. He clutched a radio receiver in his hand like a weapon. As he moved past spotters, they fell silent. They then fell in behind him in a human slipstream, following him inside.

"Come on," Estrella said. "Maybe he's going to say something."

NINE

BRONDL CALLED AN IMMEDIATE MEETING. Unlike before, the spotters fell around the tables without a word. The air was viscous and quiet. Aral took her spot at the table with Estrella at her side. Tell sat opposite them. As Brondl stepped up to his place, Tell glanced up from time to time at Aral, his eyes flashing. Brondl exchanged a few words with the two technicians, who handed him a printout and whispered something. Brondl nodded, scanned the paper, and placed it gingerly on the table.

"Nothing," the commander said to no one in particular, breaking the silence. Everyone's eyes remained on him. People seemed either afraid to speak or worried they might miss something important.

"Nothing," he repeated, this time nodding to the ComPod that lay splayed open on the table like a giant clam. "No sign of the others. No radio transmissions. No pods. Nothing on the homing receiver. So what do we do?"

A few spotters shifted in their seats, unsure if this was a rhetorical or an actual question. Brondl gave them little time to mull it over.

"I have called the CCC. They're aware of everything. Since our spotters went up, all indications suggest that all who made it up top are dead. Dead or stuck in that tube. As you can imagine, our first priority is to get them out. To get . . . my *son* out." He looked down and slid one of the teletex printouts from under a stack of paper. "According to this, there should be at least three spotters at eighteen thousand five hundred and nineteen thousand feet, assuming they're not dead. Because all radio communication is cut, we can't really know. So we have to send another team up, and right away. Leb?" He turned and addressed an imposing-looking spotter standing off to Brondl's right.

"The rescue team will be ready in thirty minutes," Leb said with a nod.

Aral let her eyes linger on Leb before turning back to Brondl.

"Thank you." Brondl looked around the tent. "According to Mira's ComPod recorder, it could take most of a day to get up there. Maybe more. If we allow a similar amount of climbing for Team Two to reach the stranded spotters, and then a half hour to disentangle them from whatever mess they're in—and this is an optimistic estimate—plus however many hours they need to get back down, that gives us a window of a day. Maybe two."

He rapped the knuckles of his right hand on the table. He seemed to be fighting off some unpleasant thought.

"And when they get back . . . " his voice trailed off. Aral glanced across the table at Tell. He sensed her gaze, looked at her, and shrugged. *I have no idea*, he seemed to say with his eyes. Aral tried to look at Estrella from the corner of her eye, but she felt compelled not to turn her head. As if doing so would somehow draw Brondl's attention.

"And when they get back," Brondl looked up. "We'll reassess. We need more information. First: are our spotters dead? Second: if they are, how? Once we figure all that out, then we can get back to our water. Assuming everything else is in order."

Nods. Grunts of approval. Whispers. Shifting in seats.

"Sir?" Aral asked. Brondl shot her a withering look. "Mm?"

"Shouldn't we wait?"

Tell looked at Aral, his face betraying worry. His eyes darted between her and Brondl.

"Wait? Our spotters are up there. What's there to wait for?" Brondl asked.

"I think what she means is," Tell said, lifting his hand to keep Aral from speaking again. Each time she asked a question, Tell worried that she might be bringing more and more of Brondl's ire upon her . . . especially now that the team—and Brondl's son—had gone missing. "What she means, I think, is that the team was planning on being back down within three days at most. They've got enough supplies for that—enough water blisters and energy gel. But yet . . . we don't know what's going on up there. All we have is one transcript, and an incomplete one at that. If there are risks, well, maybe we should give them time to finish their mission. In case, well, I mean, if it's dangerous, wouldn't it be better not to risk *two* teams?"

When he'd finished talking, Tell shot a glance at Aral. *Just follow my lead and don't push too hard*, he thought, his eyes glaring.

Brondl looked at Tell with a blank expression. He glanced around at the others as if to see if they'd heard what should've been a private conversation. With a sigh, he stepped over to the unit's radio transmitter, picked up the receiver, and pressed the transmit button.

"Triple C One, this is Brondl. Are you there?"

There was a pause, as static crackled from the radio's speakers.

"Yes, Brondl. This is Triple C One. What is it? Can you report on the reconnaissance? And the water? What's happening?"

In clipped sentences, Brondl summed up the past day and a half: cutting open the tube, the group climbing up, the cryptic message, the worrisome vital statistics. Around the table, the spotters exchanged worried looks. Aral shifted her gaze from Tell to Brondl. She felt happy her team leader had spoken up. She'd gotten in trouble plenty of times in the past for speaking when she shouldn't, but still, now, she couldn't keep quiet. There were just too many unknowns.

Brondl's radio crackled as someone from the CCC called in.

"Brondl? Brondl? Triple C One here."

"Yes? Go ahead."

"We cannot advise you to send another team up. There are too many risks. Please wait until further notice, but do proceed with your drilling."

Brondl clenched his jaw and shook his head despondently, his eyes downward. Aral had the sense that he was struggling to contain explosive emotions.

He took a deep breath and raised the radio back to his mouth. "Triple C One, my son's up there. The *team's* up there. They're in danger and may be wounded or dead. You can't really expect us to just sit here like a bunch of . . . "

"Brondl," the voice interrupted, "we hear you. We've heard you and informed the command. Let's hope for the best, but in the meantime we can't take any more risks. Your mission is to *find water*. The survival of *everyone* depends on that—not just your son. Do you understand?"

Brondl looked around at the team. Silence filled the tent. No one dared move.

"You heard it," he said. "Orders are orders. Now go find water until we hear otherwise."

TEN

TWO DAYS PASSED WITH NO NEWS.

While the spotters made progress during the day digging, drilling, shifting debris, repositioning, and drilling to a depth of sixty yards, Brondl remained inside the command post. As spotters came and went to gather tools, eat, drink, or treat minor injuries, he remained glued to the computer screen, his eyes darting across the glowing device in search of any sign, any trace, any blip that could give him a clue about the whereabouts and the wellbeing of the team and of his son. Every few minutes, he tapped the device, refreshing its display. But each time the screen revealed the same, disappointing matrix of orange and yellow pixels.

As night fell, the drilling team trudged back into the command tent, sweaty and exhausted. While Brondl sat at the tables, staring and lost in thought, the Cthonians went to their bunks, wiped themselves down with towelettes, popped in some water blisters, and ate from their rations of energy cakes made from the compacted fungus grown in the CCC. No one spoke. Tension was in the air. As they tried to relax from the day's work, no one looked at Brondl.

When Aral had finished eating, she turned to Estrella, a dejected look on her face. Estrella was just finishing her energy cake.

"You want some air?" she said at almost a whisper. As soon as she had spoken, her eyes shot to Brondl. She almost seemed afraid that he might hear her— that anything other than digging or offering a solution to the missing team would somehow be breaking unspoken rules.

"Where are you going?" Estrella asked.

"Just walking outside. Wanna come?"

Estrella nodded and stood, still chewing.

The two friends worked their way through the crowd of spotters, who were eating, massaging sore muscles, or lying down on their cots. Back at the command center tables, Brondl had looked up from the screen and was chatting softly with one of the technicians. Aral couldn't make out what the two were saying. Seeing them talk, however, she felt a wave of relief that the CCC command had called off sending up another team. *How would that even work?* she thought. *This . . . this rescue mission? What's to keep this team from falling into the same trap as the others?* Sending anyone up seemed suicidal, and she was glad Brondl was waiting. But what would happen when the waiting was up? Surely they couldn't abandon their team? And the water?

Without talking, Aral and Estrella walked straight out from the tent's door and alongside the tunnel Brondl had had erected—straight toward the massive water tube.

The two girls kept the softly glowing white material to their right. Aside from the tunnel and the tent, the night swallowed them. Behind them, men's and women's muffled voices milled about in the night—nervous, apprehensive. Aral assumed that they had relaxed and started chatting once they had seen Brondl doing something other than obsessively staring at the computer screen. Still, a palpable, nervous energy hung in the air like smog. They were almost at the limit of the reconnaissance team's supplies, at which point something would have to happen. But what? *What would the next twenty-four hours bring?*

Aral and Estrella eased farther into the darkness. Aral kept her hands in her pockets and her eyes forward. They remained half-closed and she withdrew into her thoughts.

"Never thought you'd see *this*, eh?" Estrella broke the silence.

"Hmm?" Aral shook her head and opened her eyes fully. The two were almost at the water tube, which loomed up from the sand just ten yards away.

"Remember when you took off from the cave and—"

shhhhhhhhhhhhhhBLAM!

Aral's track was cut short by an explosion twenty feet in front of her. In the dark, she could see only ill-defined grays and blacks. Sand and pebbles spewed from the ground as if a small bomb had exploded, covering her and Estrella with a fine layer of grit. At the impact, the two fell to the ground and covered their heads.

But something was wrong—strange. It was an explosion, for sure, but not an explosive device. There had been no orange flash or ear-shattering report—only a sickening and powerful *thunk*. Her heart pounding, Aral lifted her dirt-covered face and looked in the direction of the burst. No, whatever it was, it hadn't come from the ground. Something had struck the sand from above. But what?

She turned back to Estrella, who still covered her head a few yards back.

"You okay?" she asked.

Estrella looked up. "Yeah. What *was* that?"

"Lemme see."

Heart pounding from the fright, Aral turned toward the tube and lifted herself into push-up position. She kept her eyes riveted on the site of the eruption. By now her eyes had grown accustomed to the dark, but no matter how hard she looked, she could make out nothing—nothing but what looked like an irregularly shaped lump on the ground. Perhaps it was an uplift of sand, thrown up by the impact? She saw no smoke. She smelled none of the telltale odors of combustion. Had it been a meteorite? These weren't unheard of on Cthonia . . .

She inched up to a standing position. She listened. No unusual sounds stirred her suspicions. She stepped forward, every muscle tense. Estrella moved to her friend's side, and the two worked their way toward the impact site.

Closer and closer they stepped. Each girl wanted to talk to the other, but neither dared speak. Somehow, they felt as though they were being watched, listened to—that every one of their movements—their thoughts, even—were being monitored back at the control center.

"It's over there!"

"C'mon!"

"Hurry! Turn on your lights!"

A flurry of shouts from back at the tent made Aral and Estrella jump. They whirled around in the dark, their arms and fists out as if preparing to defend themselves against an attack. At that moment, Aral cursed herself for walking outside with no weapons— with no light, even. What had she been thinking? What if some hostile Ætherians had come down the tube and attacked while she and Estrella were unarmed? What if Brondl had been right after all?

Nearer the tent, Aral saw a crowd of running silhouettes moving down the access tunnel. There must've been twenty spotters running toward them. Their arms were pumping and their legs were hurtling them down the tunnel and toward the tube. Each wore a headlamp, the glaring white circles of which danced and jerked through the expanse of the tube.

"Hurry!" came a shout. Aral froze, her nerves tingling. Brondl was coming.

Stepping back, Aral looked at Estrella, whose eyes were riveted on her friend. Though the two could not make out each other's features in the dark, they seemed to read each other's minds.

"Do you think they heard it?" Aral hissed.

"They had to have."

Aral shot a look back toward the impact site.

"Do you think that was . . . "

ShhhhhhhBLAM!

Just five yards in front of them, another explosion eviscerated the tecton tunnel, sending shards of support poles and ripped tendrils of fabric hurtling outward like a monstrous, decapitated snake writhing in the death throes of the fatal blow. This time Aral and Estrella felt the detonation in their legs like a miniature earthquake that rocked the ground under their feet.

"AAAAAHHH!" Estrella shouted and stumbled backward. Aral's legs quivered as well, but she maintained her balance. The shouts in the tunnel intensified. Aral's eyes widened in horror.

"Estrella!" she screamed, her voice wavering with fear. "What is it?! Something's falling!" She looked up and rotated so that she could face the tube's fading form high in the clouds. "Do you see anything else? Watch out!"

Before Estrella could react, the noisy pack of spotters had reached the tunnel's severed end and were swarming out like ants. Their circular white lights danced around the sand and shredded tunnel like two dozen miniature searchlights. Everyone seemed to be talking at once—shouting, screaming, cursing. By now six or seven spotters hovered over the impact site, the beams of their headlamps trained on what lay at the center of a small crater. Back toward the tunnel, the other half of the group circled around the first impact site. They moved with precision and determination, as if before arriving, they had known exactly where to go. As if they had been able to home in precisely onto the locations.

Aral stepped up and gazed in horror.

There, just feet from the torn and shredded tunnel, a human body lay flat, its limbs twisted into unnatural positions. The right upper leg was bowed into an arc. The left bent at a sharp angle. The right arm was wrapped around the body as if made of rubber. The body's head seemed dented, as if it had been inflated and some of the air let out. Aral's stomach wrenched as she understood that all of the bones had been pulverized on impact. Surprisingly, Aral saw no blood. The body was intact, just distorted into sickening, unnatural shapes.

But what truly horrified Aral was not the body's mutilation.

It was that this was the body of one of their reconnaissance spotters who had gone up the tube two days before. Whoever it was had just fallen from somewhere high above.

Realizing this, Aral glanced back at the other

impact site, which she quickly saw was another body. Now that the dust had cleared, she could see some of the spotters rolling the body over onto its stomach. A wave of nausea surged through her stomach when she saw its arm flap over onto the sand like a dead fish, emitting an audible *whap*. She turned away, but her eyes fell on the scene unfolding in front of her.

Then Aral understood. The technicians in the command tent had lost track of the homing beacons once the spotters had climbed higher than the cloud. These signals must've reappeared the moment the bodies fell back below the cloud—and into a space where the signals could transmit. That's why the others had reacted so quickly. They saw the two spotters coming on the tracking screen, and they ran out to the tube to intercept them . . . just in time for the bodies to cover the distance between the cloud and the ground.

But had the two been alive or dead while they were falling?

"Oh my God," one of the spotters said, his words

clearly rising above the others' chatter. Aral stepped up to the group and peered in.

"What is it?" another asked.

"Look."

Aral shifted to her right so that she could see the body. Her blood froze.

It was Jackson—Brondl's son.

"Oh my God," the spotter repeated. Aral saw him look up at the others and wring his hands. "What are we going to do?"

"We've got to tell him . . . Is he even here?"

Some of the spotters looked around.

"No. He's back in the tent."

"Oh God . . . "

The spotter who'd identified the body stood and reached for his radio receiver, which was clipped to his shoulder.

"Aral!" a voice snapped Aral from her trance. She looked up and saw Tell's dumbfounded face looking first at her and then at Jackson's body. The headlamp lights bobbing around them gave his features a creepy, almost haunted look. Sharp, angular shadows danced over his stern expression. Aral was surprised. She hadn't seen him emerge with the others.

"What are *you* doing out here?!" he hissed, grabbing her arm and pulling her to the side, as if he didn't want anyone else to hear. She stumbled backward as he pushed, but she wrenched her arm free and stood defiantly. "I told you about running off and being gung ho. You are part of a team now!"

"I was . . . out," she said. "Me and Estrella. I just needed to . . . "

"Okay, okay," he interrupted, glancing around nervously. "Did you see this happen? Did you see . . . Jackson fall? And Mira? That's the other one." Around them the spotters spread out, absorbed in their frenzied activity. Some were examining Mira's body, while others took care to cover Jackson's body. Some were hovering over the two. Some were scanning the sky. The scene looked like a disaster area, with spotters milling about. But it was a scene that also pulsated with a sense of urgency. The spotters swarmed about frenetically, as if expecting another body to fall at any moment, even though one of the technicians off to the right kept his face plastered to the glowing orange homing screen. Seeing him gave Aral some relief. Surely he would see any more falling bodies in time to give a warning to the others so they wouldn't be crushed.

While trying to control her worries, Aral explained to Tell what she had seen. The explosion. The dust. The loud noise. He nodded absentmindedly, shifting his gaze between her eyes and the night sky. While she spoke, he continued to lift his hand to her shoulder, but she shook it off each time. With her account done, he looked her squarely in the eye.

"Come on," he said, "you need to tell this to Brondl. He has to know."

"About Jackson?" Aral's eyes widened in fear.

"About what you witnessed. You . . . " Tell fell silent, his eyes beyond the first impact site. As if on cue, the others instantly ceased talking and turned as well.

There, framed by the shredded edges of the softly glowing tent tunnel, Brondl stood dumbstruck, his eyes riveted on his son's body.

ELEVEN

EVERYONE—BRONDL, THE SPOTTERS, TELL, Estrella, and Aral—moved in a frenzy. A group of spotters ran back to the tent for two stretchers, which they brought back and used to transport the bodies to the tent. Without talking, Brondl led the group in a feverish march back to the command center. He stormed into the tent, avoiding everyone's eyes. Aral watched him move, her body frozen in fear. She had never seen him look so enraged. As she watched him, she tried to decipher his emotions. He was furious, sure, but there was something else.

His eyes glistened more than usual. He seemed to be holding back tears.

The spotters filed in and around the tables. Several others brought the now-covered bodies in on the stretchers and carried them to the dormitory section, where they disappeared from view. Brondl stepped up to the table and grabbed the radio receiver. But rather than transmit, he fingered the device in his hand and seemed lost in thought. After a few tense moments, he let the receiver drop and looked up. Aral had the impression that he was holding an intense emotion in—one that threatened any moment to explode violently to the surface.

"There you have it," Brondl said, his voice wavering. "If any of you had doubts before, I don't see how you could now. The Ætherians are hostile. Máire was right. She came to *us* for asylum. We should've listened more. But now my son's dead. Our team is dead. Our society is dying. We have no water. Judge for yourselves."

Brondl stood motionless. Aral sensed the unspoken

tension in the room. Everyone was awaiting his orders.

After a minute or so of silence, Brondl stirred and looked at his watch. He cracked the knuckles in both of his hands. He looked up.

"Cthonian spotters," he began. "It is just past midnight. I want everything in place by oh-four-hundred hours. We have explosives, yes?" he asked, turning to one of the technicians. The man opened his mouth to speak and stuttered out an answer.

"Ye-yes, but they're mining explosives, and several hundred years old at that. They're the same ones we used to dig the caves, way back when."

"Yes," Brondl said, "exactly. Well, I want those explosives around the base of that water tube. We can't wait any longer. If they're gonna attack us when we come up, then, by God, we'll force *them* down. At dawn, we cut their water. Then maybe they'll come down and negotiate. But in the meantime, we get our water back and make them pay for my . . . for attacking our team. This ends tomorrow."

———

The tent exploded into uproar. Spotters lurched left and right, everyone moving with well-rehearsed precision, each knowing exactly what they had to do. Tell led his team off to a pile of black storage containers and began unloading wire and detonators. Other spotters began pulling out little bricks of explosive and lining them up near the tent's entrance. Everyone talked at once.

As if sensing Aral's thoughts, Estrella lingered near her friend, who remained seated at the tables. She reached forward and put her hand on Aral's shoulder.

"Aral?"

No answer.

"Aral, come on, let's get to work."

Aral stood. She turned and faced her friend. She forced a smile. "Okay," she said in a defeated voice. She lifted her head and scanned the riotous tent. "Let's head to . . . " but then she stopped, her eyes riveted on the homing scanner. Estrella turned to follow Aral's gaze.

In the tumult following Brondl's orders, the technicians had left the HomScan unattended. This was the first time since they'd set up the tent and the command center that Aral had seen the device unmanned. *Did they not think it was necessary anymore?* Aral looked to her right and saw that, along with one of the other teams, the technicians were busy unfolding rolls of wire and logging something in a small metallic clipboard. They seemed to have abandoned monitoring the detector now that the decision to strike had been made. It was as if all efforts to recover the remainder of their team had been abandoned.

Around the table, the spotters were oblivious to the instrument as they moved with single-minded determination around the command center. They seemed to move with blinders on, unaware of anything other than their specific job.

And then, Aral saw it. And Estrella did, too. A small orange dot flashed on the HomScan's screen.

Twice. A continuous flashing brought the instrument to life.

The HomScan had detected another ComPod.

Only Aral and Estrella had seen it.

As if on cue, the two girls looked at each other, their eyes wide. Without speaking, they dashed over to the table and picked up the battery-powered screen, which was not connected to any other wires. Apparently thinking the device unneeded, the technicians had already unplugged it from the teletex printer. Holding it between her two trembling hands, Aral darted her eyes around the room, as if afraid that she would be caught looking at something she wasn't supposed to see. She pulled the screen close to her body, protective, guarding against others' stares, like a schoolchild protecting her exam from cheaters' eyes. She turned her eyes to the HomScan.

On the right side of the screen, a series of numbers twinkled and danced, some remaining constant, others fluctuating slightly to indicate shifting conditions in the atmosphere: TEMP 87°, BP 1012 HPA,

AH 56%, GPS 1.9706° S, 30.1044° S. The bottom right-hand portion revealed what looked to be some sort of messaging inbox: 12 unread messages. The time and date appeared at the top right corner: 0H32 6/8/93PCE. To the left of this, a battery icon flashed: 12% BATT. REMAINING.

The vast majority of the screen, however, consisted of a series of ever-widening concentric circles, like a target. The dot at the center was labeled COMMCTR 01—the command center. Each circle was labeled with a number, which Aral interpreted to be distance from the command center in meters, at five-meter increments: five, ten, fifteen, twenty, twenty-five . . . The cardinal directions formed the four sides of the screen; but rather than north appearing at the screen's top, the technicians must've reconfigured the display to show the directions in accord with the position of the tube relative to the command center. East was at the top, west at the bottom, and north and south on the left and right sides.

In the top quadrant, a lone dot pulsed. Each pulse

sent a splash of concentric light spreading out like a pebble tossed into a pond. According to the distance markers, the dot was one hundred and twenty-five meters away and to the east—directly toward the tube. A series of letters and numbers—forming some sort of identification code—hovered to the top-right of the dot: JHE 827/1—ALT 345FT/ASE.

"What do you think that means?" Estrella asked, lifting her finger to point at the code.

Aral scrunched up her eyebrows. "Can't you see?" she said, not taking her eyes from the screen. "'Alt' is the altitude. And three hundred and forty-five feet . . . that must mean that the pod isn't up *there*." She nodded upward for emphasis. "It's on the ground. It's landed! And according to these coordinates, it looks like it's near the tube!"

She lowered the screen and looked up—not at Estrella, but at the hive of activity around her.

"Should we tell Brondl?" Estrella asked.

Aral hesitated. She scanned the churning spotters.

Her face twisted in indecision. She shrugged her shoulders.

"I don't see him," she said, lifting the screen once more and looking down. "I have an idea."

Estrella narrowed her eyes. "Oh, no, is this another one of your cavalier plans to . . . "

"Look," Aral interrupted. "He's not going to listen to us. Let's at least go check. Come on!" She grabbed her friend by the shoulder and pulled her toward the tent's entrance. "Let's just go get the damn thing ourselves and bring it back! It'll take five minutes. Let's go before they get out there and start their plan!"

"Do we need anything?"

"Um . . . take those!" Aral nodded to the table where the technicians had been seated. There they had left a small set of tools that they had used to open the other pods. The tool kit was held in a type of large, folding wallet, and contained pliers, screwdrivers, Allen wrenches, a folding pocketknife, and three clamps of different sizes.

Estrella reached over and snatched up the case, folded it shut, and snapped it closed.

"And our headlamps."

"Okay," Estrella said. The two rushed around the folding curtains separating the command center from the sleeping area—Aral clutching the HomScan under her arm like a large book and Estrella gripping the oversized tool case. The dormitory area was empty. Even though it was now past midnight, no one slept. Everyone rushed about in preparation for the attack. As for Aral and Estrella, they each went to their bunks and retrieved their headlamps from their footlockers.

"Let's go," Aral said.

Estrella made for the command center, but Aral grabbed her shoulder.

"No, not that way!" she whispered. "Someone will see us."

"So what do we do? Won't they wonder where we are?"

"Maybe. But look, it's not far. We'll be back in just a few minutes. There's so much going on now, by the time they miss us we'll be back. Hopefully this one can tell us something else . . . something more, *different* from what Brondl thinks. I don't think he's doing the right thing. This way," Aral said, stepping over to the tent's edge. Estrella followed. When the two girls reached the tecton wall, they paused. Aral looked around to convince herself they were unobserved. And in one smooth movement, she bent over, scooped her hand underneath the tent's bottom edge, lifted it to knee height, and waved her friend through. Estrella dropped to all fours and crawled through the gap. Aral followed, and with only the sound of sand being kicked up against the tecton, the two disappeared into the night.

———

Within seconds, Aral and Estrella had reached the tattered end of the tunnel where the second body had landed earlier. By now the spot was deserted. The round white lights of their headlamps revealed the only sign left of what had happened earlier: the torn and frayed tecton, a seven-foot-long crater, and flurries and divots of sand and pebbles that had been kicked around by the shuffling spotters as they had investigated the scene and transported the bodies away.

When Aral and Estrella reached the end of the tunnel, they slowed to a stop. To reduce glare on the HomScan, Aral tilted her headlamp upward and kept her eyes locked on the screen. In the dark, her face glowed orange from below. The sound of the chaotic preparations back in the tent echoed through the night, overpowering the rush of water in the pipe just yards away.

"We're close," she said, looking down. As she had walked, the blinking dot and JHE 827/1—ALT 345FT/ASE had inched closer to the center of the screen, which remained situated with the coordinates of the device itself. It had not, as Aral had originally thought, been calibrated to remain locked on the coordinates of the command center.

According to the HomScan, the ComPod was five yards away. Aral looked up. That would put the pod inside the tube.

"Let's take a look," Aral said, lifting her head and tilting her headlamp back down to be in line with her line of sight.

The two girls rushed over to the tube and stepped through the dark door that had been cut out earlier. Once inside, they immediately saw the gleaming black pod wedged firmly into the ground, its oval sides covered with dents. Aral looked up. The pod must've fallen all the way down the tube. But how far? From the top? Or partway down? And whose was it? Why had it just fallen now, two days after the spotters had gone up?

Aral leaned over and placed her hands on the sides of the pod. All she had to do to remove it was to turn and lift. It slid out easily, leaving an acute, cone-shaped indentation in the sand. Keeping her headlamp trained on the ComPod, she turned it over in her hands, examining it closely. The only damage to the pod was the dents. There were no protruding wires.

"Look," Aral said, dusting off the pod. "It must've been a clean eject. Nothing's torn or broken."

"So what?"

"So . . . whoever was wearing it must've had the time to eject it. The last one had all these wires sticking out. Which could've meant that its wearer had died or been attacked—or at least not had the time to eject the pod properly."

"Okay, Detective A," Estrella sneered. "Any other clues?"

Estrella's sarcasm irritated Aral.

"Did you see how they got these things open?" Aral asked, laying the pod on the ground, latch side up. A neat seam spanned the length of the pod. Aral ran her fingernails down the seam, as if looking for some sort of latch that would trip and cause it to open. Estrella tossed the tool case over to her friend. It landed with a metallic clank, sending up a small cloud of dust.

"No, I didn't," she said. "But you're going to open it? Here? No, we really should take this back to . . . "

She stepped out of the tube and gestured toward the tent. Aral lifted her head. She had heard it, too.

"Shh!" Estrella hissed.

Aral didn't wait. She picked up the tools and tossed them back to Estrella, in the same movement scooping up the pod.

"They're coming!" she said. "Let's go! They're coming to set the explosives. Come on! Turn out your light!"

Back toward the tent, the shuffling of several dozen marching spotters made its way through the tunnel and to the water tube. But whereas before they'd been running out to intercept the pods, this time they moved coolly and with a deliberate step. As Aral stood, she marveled that the demolitions team had been able to get ready so quickly. Her stomach also churned with the fear that at any moment they would realize that the HomScan was gone, along with the tools.

They had to hurry.

As the team of spotters advanced, Aral and Estrella slipped back into the night and ran in the opposite direction: towards the command center. Aral clutched the pod to her chest while Estrella gripped the bulky tools. They clanged and rattled in their box, but the spotters heading toward the water tube took no notice. They were making enough noise to drown out the girls' racket.

When the two got back to the tent, they slipped in the same way they'd come: underneath one of the flaps several panels down from the main entrance. Just as when they'd left, no one saw them enter.

Standing at the edge of the tent, Aral scanned the command center. A few spotters had reassembled around the tables and were looking at some papers spread out in front of them. Brondl had returned and was gazing down at the documents. He rubbed his chin as one of the spotters mumbled something about one of the documents. Were they looking at the transcripts from before? Orders from command?

Maps? Aral couldn't tell. Before moving any farther, she scanned the commander's face. He still seemed to be holding in his emotions. Veins throbbed in his temples, and his jaw muscles clenched and relaxed, sending ripples up through the sides of his face.

"Sir!" Aral shouted, making Estrella jump. "Brondl!"

Brondl and the other spotters looked up in alarm. Blinded by the glaring white lights illuminating the table, Brondl held up his hand to shield his eyes. He peered into the darkness of the tent corner where Aral and Estrella had appeared. He squinted. Without waiting for her friend, Aral rushed forward, holding the pod out in front of her like a gift. Brondl recognized her. Anger flashed over his face.

"Aral!? What are you doing here?" he shouted. The others glanced at him in worry and leaned slightly away from him. Brondl jerked his head around, as if scanning the tent for someone. "Where's Tell?! You're supposed to be with the others, getting ready!"

His eyes dropped from her face to the pod. "What is that?!"

Aral ignored her fear of the general and strode up to the table. Estrella followed, but lowered her eyes to avoid the general's. When Aral reached the table, she plopped the pod down with a thud.

"Sir," she continued, speaking over strained and panting breath. Her hair fell down in front of her eyes. She pushed it out of the way and tucked it behind her ear, revealing her face, which glistened with sweat.

"Sir," she repeated. "When everyone was getting ready, we saw this on the HomScan—I mean, we saw it beeping to show that another pod had come down. Sir, we got it!"

She pointed to the pod triumphantly. Part of her hoped Brondl would be pleased with her, but part of her knew she'd disobeyed orders by running out when she was supposed to be following Tell to get ready for the demolition of the tube.

Brondl glanced back and forth between Aral,

Estrella, the pod, and the other spotters. As for the spotters, they seemed dumbstruck, frozen, their wide eyes shifting from Brondl to Aral. But they moved their heads slowly, as if to avoid being noticed by their general.

Brondl seemed to be wrestling with what to do. Open the pod? Give more orders? Punish Aral? And what about his son? Would this pod hold any more clues? He bit his lip as hundreds of contradictory thoughts flew through his mind.

He looked at Aral, his face red with fury. Silence filled the tent. He opened his mouth as if to say something to her, but held back. He took a deep, audible breath through his nose. Fifty yards on the other side of the tent's wall, the rest of the thirty-four-person team filled the night with sounds of frenetic, nervous preparation. The sound of metallic tools clanking against each other punctuated their voices. Hearing this, Brondl snapped alert and turned his head to the technician to his left.

"Open the thing. Now."

The technician nodded and reached over the table. He grabbed the pod and slid it closer.

"Sir, shouldn't we ask them to wait?" another spotter ventured, nodding his head towards the sound of the noises outside. Brondl shot the spotter a fiery glance, before looking up once more at Aral. He glanced to the table, where his orders lay . . . orders that the command itself had sent.

"No," he snapped. "We don't have any more time to fool around. Just do as you're told."

TWELVE

AS BRONDL READ THE POD'S TRANSCRIPT, NO one spoke. No one moved. All eyes were on their commander. Every few seconds, some sound from the demolition team outside made its way to the group: a voice, a shout, the mechanical *clink-clank* of munitions being secured to the tube's base. The plan was going forward.

When he'd finished reading, Brondl lowered the paper and glanced around at the others. His head nodded slowly, almost unconsciously.

"What does it say?" Aral blurted out.

Brondl's eyes darted over to her. He then shot a

withering look at Tell, as if to say, *Can't you control your spotters?*

Brondl folded the paper and laid it on top of the command's orders.

"It says the same as the others," he said, puffing out his chest. "Nothing's changed. And I have my orders from command," he waved another sheet of paper in the air. "We're cutting off their water. Maybe then they'll come down. They've killed my . . . " his voice trailed off.

Aral shot a worried look at Tell. Across the table, Estrella glared at her friend, trying to catch her attention. She felt Aral was going too far. Orders were orders, and she'd never heard of anyone speaking so openly—and bluntly—to a Cthonian general before.

"Sir?" Aral said. Brondl looked at her, but said nothing.

"Sir," she repeated. "Can we read the transcript?"

Brondl looked once more at Tell and then back at Aral.

"Can I ask you something?" Brondl asked.

"Yes," Aral answered.

"Why are you—of all spotters—so obstinate about this? Don't you know we have a mission? Guidelines?" To emphasize his point, he tapped the command's orders.

"It's just . . . " Aral hesitated, looking around. "It's just . . . don't you think . . . I mean . . . " she stuttered, looking for the right words. Her cheeks flushed in embarrassment. How could she explain here, in front of everyone, that she'd always dreamed of seeing the Ætherians, but now that they were so close, everything was spiraling out of control, and with so little information to go on?

"Sir!" a spotter's voice from the tent's entrance made her jump. Brondl turned to face him.

"Yes?"

"Sir, everything's ready."

"Just enough charges to cut the water?"

"Yes, sir."

"No more?"

"Yes, sir, but . . . "

"What is it?"

"It's just . . . these explosives haven't been used for years. And they're made for underground detonations for mining, not for aboveground."

"So what?"

"I just . . . it's that . . . I don't know how they will explode, really. What will happen. It's risky."

"Yeah, well," Brondl snapped, stepping up to the spotter. "I'll tell you what's risky: Dying from lack of water! Dying because those Ætherians have attacked! That's what's risky! And remember: it's not your place to tell *me* what to do. It's the other way around."

The spotter hesitated.

"Maybe we should wear the particulate respirators."

"Why?"

The spotter shrugged his shoulders. "For dust. Smoke. Better safe than sorry. The charges *are* focused inward toward the water tube, so all shrapnel should go inward, not out. Should be pretty small and quick, actually."

"Small and quick? Then why can't we watch? It's fifty yards away."

"Um . . . " the spotter answered, his voice trailing off. "I wouldn't recommend it."

"Yeah, well *your* recommendations don't matter, do they? I wanna see that thing come apart!"

Brondl cast a sideways glance at Aral. She thought she saw a new emotion in his eyes: vengeful rage. The thought made her burn with anger.

"Proceed," Brondl said, with a new calm in his voice.

"What?!" Aral snapped.

"You," Brondl said to Aral, "stop acting like a child. You," he said to the spotter, "begin countdown."

"Beginning." The spotter turned and ran from the tent. Aral heard him shout something to the others outside.

"Alright, everyone, you heard him. Face masks. Let's go!"

At the commander's order, the thirty-three spotters

rushed to the black equipment lockers at the side of the tent and donned face masks. Still pulling them on, they filed out of the tent to watch the severing of the tube. Laying the command's orders on the table, Brondl followed.

"Are you coming?" Tell asked. Aral looked up and saw her group leader with a face mask in his hand. "I can tell you're upset. Maybe you just want to wait in here?"

Aral shook her head. "I dunno. But I'm not a child."

"Okay, okay . . . But whatever you do," he continued, pulling the mask up and over his head. "You need to watch yourself. You don't want to get in trouble. Child or not. You're a spotter now, and that's all that matters."

"Go ahead," she said, ignoring his comment. "I'll stay here. I'll be fine. Just give me a sec."

"Suit yourself. Just remember what I said."

"Mmm."

Tell walked out with the others. When the spotters had filed out of the tent, only Aral was left behind.

No one was watching her.

Just outside the tent, she could hear the voices of four or five of the spotters discussing the charges and the countdown. Two of the voices she recognized as belonging to the two technicians. Every few seconds, Brondl let out a grunt or a short command.

She glanced around to make sure that she was alone. Seeing no one, she lunged forward and snatched up the transcript and the command's orders. Casting a furtive glance toward the tent's entrance to make sure she wasn't being watched, she unfolded the orders and read.

What she saw made her blood chill.

```
Command has received your request to
sever the tube. We cannot support this
action. You will desist immediately.
Explosives are dated and Ætherian infor-
mant reports that one of the pipes is
filled with explosive cthoneum gas that
is being piped upward. The slightest
```

spark could trigger a devastating explosion, potentially igniting massive
underground detonation. **DO NOT PROCEED**.

"Oh, my God," she mumbled. "He's going to kill us all."

Without thinking, she grabbed one of the face masks and bolted for the edge of the tent—the same edge where she and Estrella had entered earlier. She moved quickly and with purpose, sending up little clouds of sand as she shuffled away from the command center tables. She reached the edge of the tent and kneeled. She'd done this before.

"Ten, nine, eight, seven . . . " the countdown began. Silence fell in the tent.

She reached down, pulled up the tent flap, and wiggled her way outside and into the waxing morning. The tent slipped back into place, and what had been a clear voice now became little more than a muffled garble.

"Six, fihbh, fo . . . "

Once outside the tent, she ran for the parked

airship that had transported Brondl and his team from the CCC several days before.

"Threebb, twow, one . . . "

BOOM, BOOMBOOMBOOMBOOM, BOOM, BOOM BOOM!

The ground shook and the air flew from her lungs as the shockwave hit her from behind. She tumbled to the ground as if she had been hit in the back with a club.

Rolling over on her back, she gazed upwards in horror. A massive tongue of flame rocketed up the length of the water tube, sending human-sized chunks of metal flying out in every direction as it climbed. A gut-wrenching, metallic ripping sound tore through the air. Buckling like a rope that had been whipped, the pipe slowly wrenched apart and began to tumble to the ground. As it twisted and turned, geysers of high-pressure water erupted from the splitting joints.

Just as the colossal structure was beginning to dis-integrate, several piercing screams erupted from where the spotters had gathered to watch the explosion. At the same instant, a ground-shaking detonation ripped the ground apart where the pipe had been planted, sending another thunderous shockwave across the command center and a fiery mushroom cloud billowing into the sky. The ground shook with the explosion, and Aral's hearing instantly evaporated into a high-pitched, deaf squeal. The command's orders had been right. They had triggered an explosion of underground cthoneum.

Her head spinning from the report, Aral tried to pull herself from the ground where the blasts had thrown her. She had put about forty yards between herself and the tent and had nearly reached the aircraft, which remained undamaged from the blast. But she was sure that debris would be raining down any second. She had to get to cover.

Aral stood and looked back toward the pipe, but her breath failed her when she saw that it was gone. Destroyed. Tumbled to the ground in a massive pile of twisted and charred metal and piping. The only trace of its former presence was a plume of smoke that had trailed the falling structure as it collapsed. But this quickly dissipated in the morning breeze.

Silence.

The soft hush of a breeze.

She waited.

And then, without warning, a far-off *BOOM* echoed from above the clouds, exactly where the pipe had led. About a minute later, a massive, teardrop-shaped chunk of land and man-made building burst through the clouds from above like a huge rock being thrown into a pond and viewed from underwater as it burst through the surface tension of the water. The landmass must've been at least thirty yards long and twenty yards wide. At one end, the end of the mammoth tube clung to a tubular-shaped building, like some sort of octopus tentacle refusing to let go of its prey.

Aral threw her eyes downward and then back up. She stumbled backward as she realized what was happening.

The burning cthoneum gas had rocketed up and

caused another explosion high above, destroying whatever building had been connected to the pipe. And now, the building's remains were falling directly over the command center . . . directly over her. Casting her eyes straight up, Aral understood that if she didn't get into the airship, she could very well be killed by falling debris.

"Oh, my God," she muttered, stumbling backwards and turning. In her hands she still clutched the command's orders, the ComPod transcript, and her face mask. She turned and sprinted the remaining ten yards to her only source of protection.

Diving into the machine, she could only hope as the world came down around her.